The Lost Journals of Benjamin Tooth

Mackenzie Crook is a hugely diverse actor who has played a wide variety of roles, from Ragetti in the first three record-smashing, swashbuckling *Pirates of the Caribbean* films, to the wonderful character of Gareth in *The Office* and the critically acclaimed Konstantin in the Royal Court's version of *The Seagull*.

The Lost Journals of Benjamin Tooth is his second book for children.

by the same author
The Windvale Sprites

THE LOST
JOURNALS OF
Benjamin Tooth

Mackenzie Crook

FABER & FABER

First published in in 2013
by Faber and Faber Ltd
Bloomsbury House
74–77 Great Russell Street
London WC1B 3DA

Printed in England by CPI Group (UK) Ltd, Croydon, CR0 4YY

The right of Mackenzie Crook to be identified as the author and
illustrator of this work has been asserted in accordance with Section
77 of the copyright, Designs & Patents Act of 1988

A CIP record for this book
is available from the British Library

ISBN 978-0-571-29558-6

Part the First

Monday 18th April 1768

My name is Benjamin Tooth. This is my journal.

One day I will be remembered as the greatest scientist that the world has ever known and so it is my duty to mankind to record my thoughts that future generations are able to study the progress of a genius.

I am eleven years old.

Today for supper I ate of a buttock of ham with plum pudding and greens.

Tuesday 19th April 1768

Up early with the lark collecting caterpillars. I found several interesting specimens and sketched them carefully before mashing them into a pulp.

This foul puree I use to feed a hatchling bird that I rescued and am raising.

I have long known that a baby bird should be left alone, for even though it may seem abandoned its parents are usually close by, looking for food. But this particular creature did not fall from or fly the nest, it was pushed. I had been observing a pair of warblers on my way to the schoolhouse. They were a type of warbler I had not seen before and was unable to identify from any picture books. For a week I watched as the birds collected twigs and meticulously built a perfect nest in the hawthorn and lined it with feathers and grass. Soon there appeared two brown speckled eggs. The next day another. Then on the third day a surprise. Another egg, similar in colour but nearly twice the size. I soon realised that this was an intruder. The cuckoo I have heard but never spotted had found my warblers' nest.

This was the most exciting opportunity to study a phenomenon I have oft read about but never witnessed. Within very few days the cuckoo egg hatched, even though it was laid after the warbler's. Its adopted parents must have been horrified when they saw their huge offspring but set to dutifully collecting insects to fill its ever-gaping beak. The next day the first of the warblers hatched and, realising it would now have to share the supply of food, the cuckoo took action and pushed its stepbrother and the remaining eggs out of the nest. I must have arrived soon after this happened as, though the eggs were sadly smashed, the bewildered hatchling was sitting in the grass, indignantly squeaking at the injustice of it all.

The tiny, shivering creature was no more than a wrinkled skin-bag of jelly bones with a beak.

I have named the bird Lucky and he is
thriving well on his nutritious maggot-paste
diet. I take him with me to school each day in a
feather-lined teacup hidden in the pocket of my
coat. In the other pocket I keep a snuffbox of
caterpillar mash with which to feed him. I have
told nobody about Lucky, though his hungry
squawking has almost led to discovery on more
than one occasion. Miss Ormeroid is convinced
that there is a sparrows nest in the rafters of the
schoolhouse roof.

Dined today of a hot boiled green tongue with a butter pond pudding and turnips.

Wednesday 20th April 1768

I should probably say something about my circumstances so that in centuries to come scholars will have a full picture of my life and ascent to excellence.

I live at number 7 Church Street, in the market town of Mereton, with my horrible mother and ancient great-grandfather.

My father Josiah was a merchant in the fur trade and by the time I was born had done well. He decided to put most of his wealth into a ship which would travel to the New World to collect a cargo of beaver skins and sail back to England.

This one ship would have made our family's fortune and we were to move to a mansion in the country. However, the ship left Hudson Bay fully loaded but failed to arrive in Portsmouth. Fierce storms on the crossing were presumed to have claimed it but no trace was ever recovered.

On my father's death my horrible mother received a small pension and it is that which we now live off. We don't have much, my clothes are years old and threadbare, our furniture is older than Great-grandfather and we have only one servant, Eleanor, who cooks and cleans. It will be wonderful for the students of the future to think how from such humble beginnings I rose to such brilliance.

My horrible mother (I will now dispense with the prefix 'horrible' when mentioning my mother in order to save on ink, but let it be

understood that she is, indubitably, horrible)
has had a difficult life so brimful of tragedy
that it's little wonder she is a dry, cruel husk of
a woman. The accumulated horrors of having
seen seven of your children to their graves
would turn any devoted mother into a bitter,
miserly, spiteful, wrinkled old crab-trout.

The reason, I hope, that I am able to get on
in life without being so thoroughly unpleasant
is that I don't have to live with the burden of
the memories of my siblings. Four passed away
before I was even born and the other three I
hardly remember, so tender an age was I when
they each met their particular and peculiar fate.

Camilla died of the Winds, Peter of the
Leg Sweats, Eliza got the Canker and Louisa
succumbed to Dropsy. Pippa passed over after
falling down the stairs, Charley after falling

up them, and Martin died, aged five, of the Bending Disease.

My great-grandfather is a mystery. How, in a world where my poor brothers and sisters perished so young, he can live for a century or more is baffling.

Great-grandfather (I will, from hereon, dispense with the prefix 'great' when mentioning my great-grandfather, but please be assured that he is, unquestionably, great) hardly speaks any more. It is a theory of mine that we all are born with a fixed number of words to speak in our lifetime (255,507,143) and Grandfather has very few left so he uses them sparingly and wisely. Actually, not always wisely. Last month at supper he blurted out 'Cock-a-doodle-doo!' apropos of nothing. He then looked very downcast, as if he knew he'd wasted five valuable syllables, and didn't speak again for a week.

I remember a time when he used to speak more.

In the years following my father's disappearance Grandfather would tell me stories before bed. These he never read from a book but would invent from his imagination. My favourite, and one that I requested again and again, was about a tribe of tiny, flying people that lived in a far-off place where they were safe from humans.

Grandfather is also named Benjamin Tooth and has a wooden leg. A curious thing is that he will often absentmindedly scratch this wooden appendage or rub it after a long walk as though he still has feeling in it.

Most of his days are spent looking out of

the window or looking at his collection. It's
not much of a collection, to be honest. In fact
it is hard to surmise a link between each of the
objects. It comprises a spoon, a small ball of
hair, several acorns, a shoe, and various other
apparently random objects. But Grandfather
gets a lot of enjoyment from his collection,
regularly taking it out and arranging the objects
in a very specific order on the table, examining
them and cataloguing them in a notebook. He
rarely adds to the collection but when he does
he shows me his new acquisition with great
pride and I congratulate him on finding such a
beautiful example.

He is practically deaf and his eyesight
is almost gone, but his sense of smell is
astounding. He smells me coming home from
school each day and has a dish of steaming tea

waiting for me as I walk in the door.*

If I bring him a newspaper he reads it by smell, inserting one end of his 'reading straw' into a nostril and then sniffing along the lines from left to right.

He wears a periwig of the old-fashioned style and the red coat he wore at the Battle of Blenheim where he lost his leg. (He didn't *lose* his leg. It was shattered by a great shot. A grenadier, who was a butcher by trade, happened to be passing and, with his cleaver, chopped off the limb at a blow. The grenadier subsequently went on to become Surgeon General of the whole army. Or so the story goes.)

I attend the dame school at Stonebridge, which is a three-mile walk across the fields from my house. The schoolmistress, Miss

* I do not have a particularly pungent odour.

Ormeroid, is a crotchety old hag who has no more idea of how to teach children than I do of making lace. I already feel I have learnt as much from her as I can. We spend hours reciting aloud number tables or verses from the scriptures. We also have to copy out and commit to memory whole chapters from Miss Ormeroid's (to the best of my knowledge) *only* book. *A Practical Discourse on the Benefits of Serious-Minded Contemplation of Various and Diverse Philosophies* by the Reverend James Diggens is without doubt the dullest book ever written. I worry that my brain is being filled with these utterly mind-numbing passages, that it will soon have no space left and something really important will be pushed out, like how to stand up. I fear I will memorise one sentence too many, forget how to stand up and just crumple to the floor.

For the past two years I have been secretly collecting woodworms from the old timbers in our attic and pushing them into the spine of the confounded volume before school. However, they must find it as boring as I and soon crawl out in favour of the leg of Miss Ormeroid's desk. At least one day the desk might collapse, which will provide a momentary distraction.

(The woodworms are the larvae of the death-watch beetle. These tiny insects make a clicking noise that I sometimes hear on very still and quiet nights. This sound is thought by some to be a premonition of a death in the house. I imagine this must be a superstition although it must be said that Death has been a constant visitor to our home. He barges in without invitation and never wipes his feet.)

Once a week on a Thursday we are visited
by Mrs Butterford who comes to instruct us
in Natural History and Botany. It is these
Thursday lessons that I live for and that are my
greatest joy. The weather being fair we leave the
confines of the schoolhouse and venture into
the surrounding countryside. There we collect
specimens, one day catching butterflies with a
net, another day dipping in ponds and streams
or counting the different species of tree in a
hedgerow. (They say you can tell the age of a
hedgerow by the number of species growing
in it: a new species will establish itself every

hundred years. If this is true, the hedge that borders the eastern side of Farmer Gantry's pasture has been there since the time of the Romans.)

If the weather is inclement we stay at school and write up our findings, pressing flower and leaf samples, mounting butterflies and beetles, and painting watercolours from the sketches taken in the field.

Mrs Butterford is a wonderful painter and has taught me much. Her renderings of wild flowers are as freshly delicate as the real thing, such that I imagine I can smell their perfume.

It is during these study periods that I dream of one day being a great naturaller and fellow of the Royal Society, travelling to far-off lands, discovering new species of flora and fauna and bringing them back to the astonishment of the scientific community.

To achieve this dream though I would need to win a place at university and that is as likely to happen as Grandfather's leg growing back. To study at university one needs much wealth and much wealth is something my family has very little of.

Nevertheless I will continue my studies lest a rich benefactor should one day decide to patronise me and I can take my place amongst the hallowed stones of Oxford or Cambridge.

Saturday 23rd April 1768

Today I helped the Archdeacon to drain and clear the fish pool without the gardens of the deaconry. It is thought that the pond has not been cleared these fifty years and it was choked with reeds and lilies. The pond is fed from the south by a dyke, which we stopped off with sandbags. Then, stretching a net over the channel to the north, we widened it with shovels allowing the water to drain away. It was dirty, smelly work but fun!

The Archdeacon is a capital fellow and insisted upon helping. Indeed he seemed to relish the opportunity to cast off his clerical robes and wallow around in the mud and sludge dressed solely in a pair of old britches.

Each time a fish was caught in the net he would hold it above his head with a cry of 'Lo! Another of God's gold!' or 'Holy mush!'

By midday the pond was half-emptied and we sat on the bank to eat our lunch.

We got back to work and the remaining

fish were removed in time for Mr Whitbourne
the monger to collect them and take them to
market: in total a dozen large eels, two dozen fat
roaches, the same of perch and five handsome
tench. The archdeacon made me a present of a
brace of eels for my help.

The day nearly over I arranged to come back
on the morrow to stop up the gap and re-flood
the pool. It was only then that we noticed a
movement in the mud. Something large was
pushing through the shallow water left in the
bottom of the pond. With a twinkle in his eye
the archdeacon turned to me, cried, 'Here be
monsters!' and leapt into the ditch. There, with
great effort, the two of us wrestled from the silt
a magnificent, gigantic beast of a catfish, seven
feet from head to tail with coral rings in its fins!
I have never seen anything like it.

Dined tonight of a pigeon pudding and green salad.

Mother very bad with a Swelled Face. Dr Lamprey came and bleeded her with leeches.

Thursday 28th April 1768

Today I discovered a most rare and beautiful creature.

Her name is Izzy Butterford and she is the daughter of Mrs Butterford who teaches us of a Thursday and quite the gentlest and kindest thing on Earth. She has joined Miss Ormeroid's school and sits next to me in class.

Today Mrs Butterford issued us all with butterfly nets and took us out to the meadow. Izzy refused to join us in mounting the butterflies we caught but instead painted them in the meadow and set them free. Even more extraordinary (and I wouldn't have believed it had I not seen it with mine own eyes) she sat on a tuffet with her paints beside and paper on lap while a butterfly sat patiently on her skirts. When she had done she said, 'There now, it is finished, thank you, goodbye,' whereupon the butterfly fluttered its wings and was gone! I might have thought this a coincidence but,

Journal, I saw it three times!

Izzy is almost as good an artist as her mother and knows the names of all the birds and flowers. I so wanted her to think well of me that I broke my vow and showed her the baby bird in my pocket. She was enchanted and asked if she could help look after it. I of course agreed and she is to come to the house Monday next after school.

Dear Journal I cannot tell you but she is the prettiest maid and I am truly smitten.

This even I shall eat a great deal of cheese that I may dream tonight of sweet Izzy Butterford.

Mother abed with Fatigue of the Blood.

Friday 29th April 1768

The cheese I ate made me dream of great fat
frogs with human hands.

There is a shop in Stonebridge that draws
me to it every time I pass. It is an establishment

called Gadigun's Taxidermology: Stuffing, Embalming, Preserving, Mounting. Behind the grimy windows stuffed animals are frozen in action, real animals in realistic poses caught in a moment of time. I would like to learn how to do that one day.

Monday 2nd May 1768

Today Izzy Butterford came with me back to Church Street after school.

I took her to the woodshed where I have built the nesting box in which Lucky roosts at night. I have made it comfortable with moss but Izzy insisted that 'such a perfect darling should not have to sleep in such a cobwebby hovel' and before long she had me sweeping the shed and garlanding the walls with posies of flowers. Then I had to lay a fragrant carpet of lavender and rose petals that the smell of damp would not offend his 'pretty nostrils'. I felt sure that Lucky eyed me with a sneer as if to say, 'What creature is this that has you sprinkling whimsy like a bridesmaid?'

Izzy left for home at five of the clock and though I was sad to see her go I am glad she left before evening as I feel sure she would have had me singing lullabies to send the bird to sleep.

Tuesday 3rd May 1768

Today I showed Izzy the warblers' nest. She was at first excited but soon became melancholy when she saw how hard the warblers have to work to keep their foster child fed.

'Oh how can such beautiful creatures behave so cruelly to one another?' she lamented. I told her there was no room for kindness or sentimentality in the struggle for life but she called me 'unfeeling and cold'.

The cuckoo chick is now a monster. It has outgrown the tiny nest and sits atop it like a turkey on a flowerpot. The warblers will be looking forward to the day it fledges and they can get some respite from the continual gathering of food. They must surely be put off raising children for good by that greedy parasite who bears no family resemblance.

Thursday 5th May 1768

Lucky is almost fully fledged and Izzy has said that I should set him free.

I reluctantly own that she is probably right. I had thought that he could be my pet and companion but small birds cannot be tamed like a jackdaw or a jay and, unless I kept him in a cage, he would eventually fly away.

Izzy thinks that we should take him far away, for he is so trusting that if he stayed in Mereton he would fall prey to a cat before long. I will keep him a few days more until I am satisfied that his wings are strong and he can find his own caterpillars. Then I will take him to Windvale Moor, a wild and isolated area several miles to the south-west of here.

For supper Eleanor served up a piece of pork with peas and a rhubarb and gooseberry pye so sour it almost took the enamel off my teeth.

Mother abed with Yellowing of the Elbow.

Friday 6th May 1768

I had the idea today of a cart or carriage that needs no horses to pull it. It will carry its own source of energy, its 'motor', along with it and therefore be free of the restrictions of a horse. It could speed along and make the journey from London to Birmingham in a day.

I sketched out the plans for such a carriage using a windmill as the engine. I predict that in the future every household will have one.

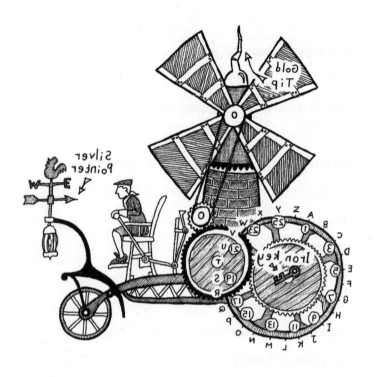

Saturday 7th May 1768

Tomorrow Izzy and I will go to Windvale Moor and set Lucky free.

Sunday 8th May 1768

I set out early on the road to Windvale and soon met Izzy by the millpond where she was waiting for me as arranged. We walked a mile or two before we were able to hitch a ride with some workers who were going to the moor to gather furze. It was a beautiful sunny day and we lay back in the cart and watched a skylark climb to impossible heights. A tiny speck above us, its song the faintest of trills, it stayed awhile on quivering wings and then dropped like a pebble from the sky.

I have seen this behaviour many times but Izzy worried that the lark had been shot. I assured her it was safe and that they spread their wings in the nick of time to arrest their fall and land safely on the ground. Izzy asked why they do this but I could only reply that I thought it was for sheer joy. Not very scientific but she seemed happy with the answer.

After a few hours we were nearing the moor and so parted company with the furze gatherers to walk the last mile.

Windvale Moor is even more beautiful than I remembered and today the air was strewn with threads of glistening gossamer drifting over the grass. We sat and watched the pipits and warblers making the most of the summer bounty and then set Lucky in a patch of furze and retreated to watch through my telescope. Before long he was flitting this way and that, snatching insects from the air and searching the brush for caterpillars. It felt good to have given him his freedom and I am happy that he will thrive on the moor.

At one point, as we watched, Izzy spotted a pair of huge dragonflies. They were some way off but looked to be quite twice the size of any I had seen before. At first I thought they must be swallows but the glimpse I caught through my telescope before they disappeared confirmed they were certainly not birds.

I will keep my eyes peeled for further sightings.

As we made ready to leave Izzy noticed a lone figure some half a mile away who also seemed to be scanning the moor through a glass. I watched him for a time and as I did he turned and looked towards us. For a brief minute we stood observing each other. It was a strange, unnerving feeling after such a joyous day and Izzy asked that we might leave for home.

Thursday 12th May 1768

Today being the day when Mrs Butterford
teaches us, I decided to show her my sketches of
the warblers that I did while they were making
their nest. She was interested but was uncertain
of the species, saying they resembled reed
warblers or willow warblers but weren't enough
like either for her to say for sure. I worry now
that Lucky was an entirely new species that I
have let slip through my fingers. Oh why did I
let Izzy persuade me to release him?

The next chance I get I will go back to the
moor to try and find him again.

Mother abed with Teeth Cramps.

Sunday 15th May 1768

Today I had a baffling encounter with a stranger
on the moor that has left my head swimming
with questions.

I spent the day on Windvale searching in vain
for Lucky or one of his kin. I spotted both reed
and willow warblers aplenty and am convinced
that Lucky was neither.

But as I was searching I saw again the
mysterious figure that Izzy and I observed
last Sunday. He was once more alone and
apparently without bag or possessions,
standing with his glass scouring the moor.

What was he looking for? The same thing
as me?

I quickly hid behind a bluff and watched him
awhile unnoticed. Every time he looked towards

me I ducked down out of sight.

Crawling along the bluff I was able to reach a place where I could sit and observe the landscape whilst remaining hidden and this I did for an hour or so.

I decided at length to change position but as I turned to move, suddenly he was there in front of me. He was standing twenty paces off and pointing at me, shaking his finger.

'What are you doing?!' he shouted. 'What do you want?!'

I didn't know what to answer lest, as I suspected, we were looking for the same thing.

'Nothing,' was my eventual (and brilliant) reply.

'LIAR!' he screamed, taking a few paces back and brandishing his bony finger at me like a musket. 'What's your name?'

'Tooth,' I answered. 'Benjamin Tooth.'

At this he flung up his arms and collapsed to the ground where he proceeded to writhe and moan as though in agony. I approached warily but he raised his hand toward me.

'Stay away!' he shrieked. 'STAY! Step no closer! I relinquish it! It's yours!' He was reaching into his coat, scrabbling about in the pockets, and was about to draw something out when I said, 'Sir, I was watching for birds on the moor. I mean you no harm nor want anything from you.'

He lay stone still for a moment and I took a step closer.

'STAY!' he howled again, holding up his palm.

I stood and said not a word. Slowly he rolled away from me then looked back over his shoulder.

'Do you know me?' he asked.

'No, sir, not as I can recall.'

'Think back!'

'To when?'

'To fifty years past!'

'Sir, I am but eleven years old.'

He lay still on the grass, eyeing me suspiciously, and then slowly, very slowly gathered his coat skirts around him, got to his feet and turned towards me.

I took a step.

'STAY!' he cried, pointing at my feet.

Now was the first time I got a proper look at the fellow and a properly strange-looking fellow he was. It is hard to say how old he was, possibly not yet thirty, but gaunt and haunted. His skin, translucent and shiny, was pulled taut over his bones and looked as though he had been scrubbed rather too vigorously with a pumice. His eyes, a ghostly pale blue, protruded from his skull with an expression of abject terror as he watched me and his thin lips were drawn back in a grimace revealing a set of white teeth too large for his head. He had the appearance of a freshly skinned rabbit.

His clothes were old. Not just shabby and threadbare but of an old style many decades out of fashion. His hair of a sickly yellow colour was piled on top of his head like custard on a pudding.

'Tooth?' he said at length.

'Yes, sir, Benjamin Tooth.'

'And eleven years old?'

'Yes, sir.'

'No more?'

'I'll be twelve years this Michaelmas.'

He stood considering this for a few moments before he forced what I can only think was intended to be a smile, though it hardly differed from the grimace he had worn previously.

'Well then, young Tooth,' said he, 'you must forgive me, I mistook you for somebody else. Let me introduce myself. My name is Cupstart. Farley Cupstart.'

At this he took a few slow steps closer as though creeping up on a nervous animal that was likely to take flight at any sudden movement. Seemingly at a loss for anything else to say, he straightened up and took a deep breath whilst looking out over the moor.

'Birds, you say?'

'Yes, sir.'

'Yes, me too. I have been watching for *birds* just the same as you. *Birds*. Fascinating creatures. And tell me, young *Tooth*, have you spotted any?'

'Why yes, sir, many, and of several kinds.'

'Indeed? Indeed!' He nodded his head vigorously to indicate that he knew *exactly* what I was talking about. 'And have you spotted anything . . .' he leant in close, '*unusual?*'

'Not really, sir,' I answered, 'though I saw a harrier, which are normally elusive.'

He nodded thoughtfully and stroked his whiskerless chin.

'Have you spotted anything unusual, Mr Cupstart?' I asked, at which his eyes snapped suspiciously back to me.

'Like what? What do you mean?'

'Well . . . like a harrier?'

'Ah, yes, no, nothing out of the ordinary. Just a few . . . chickens.'

'Chickens, sir?'

'Yes, chickens. Chickens are birds, are they not?'

'Yes, sir.'

From this it was not difficult to deduce that Farley Cupstart was not a birdwatcher of any great expertise. Neither was he a good actor for he then made an unconvincing show of trying to remember something.

'Tooth . . . *Tooth*, you say?'

'Yes, sir.'

'Tell me, young *Benjamin Tooth*, would you, by chance, live in Mereton?'

'Why yes, sir,' I replied, genuinely surprised.

'In Church Street?'

Again I answered in the affirmative.

'Ah, then all becomes clear!' said Mr Cupstart. 'I was once a great friend of one of your ancestors, many, many years ago before you were even born.'

'Really, sir?'

'Oh yes, *very* great friends and I often visited this relation of yours at the old house in Church Street. Before you were born, you understand?'

'Indeed, sir?'

'Yes indeed! And do you know . . .' again he tried to pretend that the remembrance had only just occurred to him, 'I left something with that relation of yours (many years ago) and I wonder if it is still at the house?'

'What sort of a something?' I asked and with that he started to fish around again in his coat pockets, eventually withdrawing a crumpled piece of paper and a short stick of charcoal. Moving over to a flattish rock he began to sketch something on the paper.

When finished he held it up to show me.

'Does this mean anything to you?' he asked.

The drawing resembled a large insect with
veined wings and a fish's tail. He leaned in
close to study my reaction and for the first
time I noticed his smell, strangely aromatic
like frankincense or bergamot, but not fresh,
rather stale and musty as clothes sprinkled with
scented oils and left in a drawer for years and
years. The drawing meant nothing to me and
he must have seen it in my face as he shook the
paper and pointed at it.

'Think, boy! Have you seen this before?'

'No, sir,' I replied. 'I don't think I have. What
is it?'

'It's mine!' he cried, forgetting for a moment
his faux-friendly demeanour. 'And I want it
back!' He checked himself and allowed the

toothsome grin to spread across his face like mould.

'Look again . . .' he said, 'try and remember. Have you seen anything in your house at Church Street that resembles this drawing? Perhaps on a mantelpiece or at the back of a cupboard?'

'Not as I can think of, sir.'

His brow furrowed and he slowly folded the paper before putting it back in his pocket.

'Have a look around your house, boy, and see what you can find. Perhaps it is hidden in a closet or beneath the floor. Look carefully, for if you can locate it I will pay you handsomely for it. It is mine, you understand, and it is of no worth to anybody else but I would dearly like to see it again. It holds great sentimental value for me which is why I would reward you if you could return my property to me.'

He turned to look out across the moor.

'Do you go to school, boy?' said Cupstart, staring dreamily into the distance.

'Yes, sir, to Miss Ormeroid's dame school at Stonebridge.'

'Then I shall meet you tomorrow on your way to school and you can tell me what you have discovered.'

He was still gazing across the moor in a trance as I got up to leave but then snapped to attention and called after me, 'Tell nobody that you met me! It will be our secret and when you are rewarded it will be a sweet surprise for your family! Do you agree?'

'Yes, sir,' I said.

'Until tomorrow then, young Benjamin Tooth!'

I left him sitting on the grass and started for home.

I arrived back to find Mother in the foulest of moods with a face like a bag of smashed crabs. Eleanor, our maid, had taken the day off suffering from Oily Eyes and the house was in a mess. I volunteered to clear up thinking it might be a good opportunity to poke around in some nooks and crannies and look for the object of Mr Cupstart's enquiry. This did not occasion any grateful thanks from Mother but rather a sneer and 'A maid's work is all you're good for,' but I'm used to her vitriol. It's like bile off a duck's back.

As I tidied away I looked in all the old storage cupboards but with not much of an idea what I was looking for. Cupstart had not told me what the drawing represented, from what it was made or even its size.

So here am I trying to decipher these most intriguing of events. I shall recall the drawing as best I can and sketch it now before the memory fades.

Monday 16th May 1768

I have awoken this morn with an ill and uneasy feeling that Farley Cupstart is a villain who is up to no good.

I am ashamed to think that his promise of financial reward had me snooping around like a burglar in my own house.

If he is there this morning as he said he would be I will ask outright what is the object he seeks and if he won't say I will tell him I want no further part in it.

Later

After I penned this morning's brief entry I set out to school with a will of iron. I turned left out of Peter Thorington's yard and there, a hundred yards along the lane, leaning against the gate of Church Farm, waited the menacing figure of Cupstart, waving and smiling his counterfeit grin as if delighted to see me again.

'Good morrow to you, young Tooth!' he shouted out when I was still some way off. He looked as though he wanted to rush forward to meet me but managed to resist the urge and remained leaning against the stile in what he imagined was a casual attitude. I approached.

'Greetings! Greetings!' He took my hand in his and vigorously pumped it up and down. His skin was so soft and cool that at first I thought he was wearing velvet gloves. It was all I could do to stop myself recoiling with a shudder.

'I see you have your school satchel about you,

young Benjamin,' said he. 'Might I be allowed to hope that within is my property that you have found and are returning to its rightful owner?' His creepy leer did not last long and was replaced by a forbidding glare as I replied in the negative.

'You found nothing?'

'Nothing, sir.'

'Did you look?'

'Yes, sir.'

'Then you did not look hard enough!' All traces of his feigned good nature evaporated now as he grabbed me by the throat with one hand and tore my bag from my shoulder with the other. He emptied the contents of my satchel on the path and kicked at them.

'Where is it?!' he screamed with rage.

'I found nothing, sir!' I could hardly breathe

for his hand, though creepily soft, had a vice-like grip on my neck. 'I promise!'

'Did you look everywhere, boy?' he hissed.

'Everywhere but my grandfather's room as he was already abed,' I replied with difficulty.

At this Cupstart stopped and released me. He thought for a moment.

'Your grandfather, you say?'

'Yes, sir,' I replied. 'Well, he is not my grandfather but my great-grandfather, on my father's side.'

This information seemed to strike Farley Cupstart like a bolt of lightning. He performed a series of dance steps: walking off two paces, turning back, slapping his forehead, spinning on the spot, looking to heaven and then coming in close enough that I could smell his breath (mothballs and nutmeg).

'Your *great*-grandfather?' he said slowly. 'And would his name, by chance, also be . . . *Benjamin Tooth*?'

'Yes, sir.'

Cupstart seemed to be calculating something inside his head.

'Then it is true,' he whispered to himself. He looked at me sideways through narrow eyes and seemed to be regretting his former violent behaviour.

'You must not mind me, young Benjamin, or may I call you Ben?'

His suddenly friendly demeanour did not fool me for one minute but, afraid of being throttled again, I agreed.

'I did not mean to frighten you, young Ben,' he continued. 'It was merely a test. Yes! A test to see if you are a brave young man! And you passed that test! Well done! And now we can be friends again! Agreed?'

He leant in close once more and very deliberately asked, 'What does your great-grandfather *look* like?'

'Why, sir, he looks like . . . *Grandfather.*' I
didn't know how specific he wanted me to be.

'Does he look . . . *like me?*'

'No, sir, he is an old, old man.'

'But does he look young . . . for his age?'

'No, sir, he looks every day as old as his years.'

Cupstart rubbed his smooth cheek.

'Wrinkled skin?'

'Like a prune, sir.'

'White hair?'

'What little there is left is as white as snow.'

'Teeth?'

'One, sir.'

'Ironic. Eyes?'

'Dim and cloudy, sir.'

With that Cupstart moved away and paced
up and down muttering to himself, 'What does
this mean? What *can* this mean?' as I collected

my things and replaced them in my satchel. Suddenly it was as though I had become invisible to him, as though he had no further need for me, and he did not raise his eyes as I edged around the fence and headed off in the direction of Stonebridge. On the other side of the paddock I turned and looked back. Cupstart was still pacing and evidently still talking to himself for he was gesturing and gesticulating to the surrounding countryside in a most animated fashion.

All day at school I was distracted and could not concentrate on my work. Miss Ormeroid noticed and hauled me out in front of the class to recite some piece of nonsense from her book of tedium.

At home time I rushed out and hurried back

towards Mereton where I was presented with a
most distressing scene.

Mother was in the best parlour serving tea
in our best china to none other than Farley
Cupstart.

'Aha!' he cried when he saw me. 'Young
Benjamin home from the schoolhouse! You
see I have dropped in for a visit with your dear
mother!'

I was as polite as I could be but a feeling of
dread was knotting my insides.

'Mr Cupstart is an old friend of Great-
grandfather,' said my mother. 'He has popped
in to pay his compliments but unfortunately
Grandfather has gone to visit his aged friend,
Mr Pyecrust, at Inglesea.'

'No matter!' said Cupstart. 'I can visit another
time, and what's more, your grandfather's

absence has given me a chance to meet your charming and, if I may be so bold, *fragrant* mother.'

At this a nauseating smile broke out across his face like a pox and he leant forward and patted my mother's hand.

Journal, I nearly puked.

It was made worse by my mother batting her eyelids, giggling like a moron and softly slapping the villain's wrist.

'Oh, Mr Cupstart,' she simpered, 'you really are a very *naughty* man!'

I made my excuses and fled.

Cupstart left about twenty minutes later and I watched through the window as he walked away talking to himself.

Almost immediately he had gone I heard Mother downstairs clattering around and banging cupboard doors. On enquiring what she was doing she replied that she was looking for something and it was none of my business.

Later, when Grandfather returned home he stopped inside the door and sniffed the air. A dark shadow crossed his face and he stalked slowly from room to room, lingering awhile in each. He stayed longest in the best parlour and when he came out he was wearing an expression of great concern. He looked accusingly at my mother but she offered nothing and so I too kept quiet about our visitor.

But Grandfather knew. And by his reaction I do not believe that Farley Cupstart was as great an acquaintance as he claims to have been.

Tuesday 17th May 1768

This morning Grandfather surprised us all by writing a message on a piece of paper.

It said:

Today I am 111.

We were thrilled. We congratulated him on reaching such a grand old age and wished him a happy one-hundred-and-eleventh birthday.

He shook his head and pointed at the note again. We realised that in fact it said: Today I am *ill*, so we called the doctor who diagnosed Nervous Thumbs and applied a poultice.

Grandfather then stayed the rest of the day in his room.

After school today I walked with Izzy. I toyed
with the idea of telling her about Farley
Cupstart but thought better of it and instead
amused her with various topics about which
I know an awful lot. She didn't say much but
seemed content to just listen to my scintillating
discourse. She told me she had read that
yawning increases the flow of blood to the brain
and improves the understanding of interesting
conversation. I offered to accompany her all the
way home but she said she needed some time to
think about the many fascinating things I had
told her. I bade her farewell by the old round-
towered church and headed back to Mereton.

As I came around the corner into our street
I stopped short as I spotted the familiar lanky

figure of Farley Cupstart at the door talking
to Mother. I ducked out of sight behind a wall
and watched for a moment. Cupstart had one
hand up on the doorframe and was leering
horribly as Mother laughed and blushed like
a little girl. Then, all at once, what I believe
was a teacup came flying through the open
door and hit Cupstart hard on the temple. He
yelped and staggered back into the flowerbeds
as Grandfather came barrelling out brandishing
his walking stick. Cupstart tripped over the
sweet peas and was scrabbling back on to his
feet as Grandfather (with astonishing agility for
a monopod) hopped across the path and gave
him an almighty kick up the azaleas.

I stayed well back and hidden and watched
as Farley Cupstart hotfooted it up the road
cursing back towards the house. Grandfather

stood glowering after him and then turned and went inside. I waited a few moments before coming up the path but when I entered the house Mother was sulking in her bedchamber, Grandfather was shut in his room and the whole house was quiet.

Grandfather didn't reappear for the rest of the day but now, past eleven of the clock, as I sit here writing, I can hear him moving about downstairs.

Perhaps I should go and check that he is all right.

I have just returned from Grandfather's room where he spoke to me more words than he has said for years. I must write them down before I forget:

An ill wind bloweth, my boy, around this house.

Age disguised as youth.

Searching for life with dead eyes.

It will bring no good to the little people.

I must return what is theirs.

I asked him to explain but I fear he has used up the last of his words.

Thursday 19th May 1768

I am worried for Grandfather as this morning he is missing from the house and doesn't look to have slept in his bed. He will occasionally go for walks when he has something on his mind. Curse Farley Cupstart.

Later

A bad day.

To school as usual and then home to find the world turned upside down.

Mother had been out all morning on various errands and while she was away the house was broken into and ransacked. Cupboards were emptied and the contents strewn across the floor. Dressers and furniture were pulled over, curtains and wall hangings ripped down. Grandfather's room was the worst and had been thoroughly turned over. Even the floorboards had been prised up and lay splintered all around. It looked as though the place had been torn apart by cannon shot.

Mother was in the parlour being comforted by neighbours whilst Mr Wooten, the local sheriff and Justice of the Peace, asked her questions. In a rare show of affection Mother threw her arms towards me and cried, 'Oh my poor boy! What have they done? What have they done to our home? We are ruined! We shall have to live on the streets and beg for food!'

The justice tried to calm her down and assure her that we were not at all ruined but that, though the house was in a dreadful state, nothing seemed to have been taken and everything could be fixed up as it was before.

It was only then that the obvious occurred to me. The shock was at first so great I had not put my mind to who could be responsible. But at the realisation that not a thing had been taken, not the cutlery, plate, linen, china, I knew that only one person could have done this: Farley Cupstart.

Nobody thought to ask me if I had any

suspicions and so I kept quiet. The truth is I am greatly afraid of that man and what he is capable of. I don't know his motives but it seems he will stop at nothing to get what he seeks and has no morals or conscience to speak of.

I am sitting in my room once more writing this entry. It is late. I spent the evening with various friendly townspeople trying to get the house back into some semblance of order. Some of the furniture was smashed and has been taken away to be repaired, and the carpenter will come on the morrow to replace the lifted floorboards, but otherwise we were able to make the house habitable again.

I think Mother is finally asleep after hours of distressed wailing and predicting doom for us all.

One more dreadful thing that I can hardly

bring myself to mention is that Grandfather is still missing. At least I know that he left before the house was raided, otherwise I would be afeared that Cupstart had kidnapped him. I am trying to comfort myself with the thought that he may have gone to visit Mr Pyecrust in Inglesea again. Perhaps I will borrow a horse and ride over that way in the morning.

But now I must try to sleep.

Friday 27th May 1768

I have not written for a week or more.

This house has become a place of misery. Mother's hair has turned completely white and she sits weeping and wailing and bemoaning our bad fortune.

Grandfather is still missing. I travelled to Inglesea Saturday last but found that he had not been to visit his old acquaintance nor had anybody heard anything of him. I worry that he is gone for good and that Farley Cupstart drove him away.

Neither have I seen hide nor hair of that villainous gentleman.

It is the fear of encountering him again that has kept me from Windvale Moor but I have become strangely drawn to that wild and lonely place and will soon go back to clear my mind of cobwebs. The moor holds some kind of answer, I am positive. I go there to look for my warbler but really I am searching for something I cannot name. It is becoming an all too familiar feeling.

Mother abed with Flatulence.

Sunday 19th June 1768

I travelled to Windvale Moor today to clear my head and think. Instead I have returned with my head in a mess and my thoughts more foggy and confused than before.

It was with great trepidation that I took my first steps into that sea of grass lest I should again meet with Farley Cupstart. I was soon confident that I was alone and set to observing the fauna of the moor through my telescope. Before long a sense of calm enveloped me and I started to relax for the first time in many days.

This did not last.

I soon spotted what looked like a reclining figure in the grass. I watched for a while but the shape did not move and indeed some rabbits grazing close by told me that this was not a person as I first thought. Reassured that I was not about to stumble upon a sleeping Farley Cupstart I made my way towards what I soon saw to be a pile of old clothes.

At twenty yards I stopped in my tracks and my blood ran cold as I recognised my grandfather's faded red coat. There on the ground, not my grandfather, but his clothes lay in a heap like the scarf and hat of a snowman that has melted away. There were no rips or tears, no bloodstains or evidence of foul play, just the garments and his wooden leg abandoned in the grass. His belt was still secured about his coat but all the buttons were missing. I looked around, searching in among the rocks and boulders of the overhang.

I called out, but my voice drifted off over the moor and was not answered.

I admit, Journal, that I sat down next to the clothes and wept, for though I could explain nothing I was quite certain that I had seen the last of my dear grandfather. It was only when I reached out and took up the wooden leg that I noticed the straps which held it in place were undone and as I turned it over the top fell away. Grandfather's leg was hollow and unscrewed to reveal a secret chamber, but there was nothing within.

One last thing. As I sat contemplating the mystery of what had happened to my aged kin I spotted two of those huge dragonflies skimming away from me across the moor.

Part the Second

Friday 14th August 1772

My name is Benjamin Tooth. This is my journal.

It has been four years since last I wrote.

My circumstances have changed and I no longer live in Mereton with my family. In fact I no longer have any family. I am the last surviving Tooth.

After my grandfather disappeared life at Church Street became unbearable. It is strange now to think that the old man who hardly uttered a word, who shuffled about in his own twilight world, was the fragile glue that held my family together. His care and our devotion to him was the only tenderness that existed in our home and once he had gone (I still know not where) all pretence of family affection dried up.

My mother had never cared for me. She all but admitted it herself. And once I was the only thing left in her life she quickly allowed herself to contract something terminal and died within the year.

I wasn't much aggrieved. I didn't care much for her either.

However, the ill-tempered whelk saw fit to set my life on a miserable trajectory before she passed away and though I am now almost sixteen I can still feel her clammy fingers on my shoulder pushing me in directions I do not wish to go or at the very least holding me back from taking my own chosen route.

I'll keep it brief.

Not long after our house was ransacked my mother decided that my schooling was leading nowhere and that I should leave immediately and find a trade. My father's meagre pension was running out and we needed money.

In Stonebridge, not far from the schoolhouse, is a taxidermist's shop. From an early age I was always fascinated by this shop and would stop whenever I could and peer in through the window at the stuffed animal displays. The taxidermist, a man by the name of Pansas Gadigun, specialised in mounting creatures in dynamic poses as though they had been frozen in time. A weasel in the front window was locked in an eternal battle with a viper, the snake twisting around its body and preparing to strike. The weasel was baring its teeth, and where its claw had punctured the reptile's skin a drop of crimson blood oozed out. A magnificent red fox had been turned to a statue in the act of escaping with a pheasant,

and a kestrel was caught at the moment of
diving on an unsuspecting vole.

By cupping my hands around my eyes I could
see past the window displays and into the dark
interior of the shop where jars of fluids and

boxes of wire and tools were crowded on to shelves.

At one point Mr Gadigun got married and soon after his window displays took a strange turn as the animals began to wear clothes and were set in human situations. A pair of dormice played croquet, a hedgehog and a ginger kitten drank tea and a mole in blacksmith's overalls hammered tiny horseshoes at his anvil. This one confused me. Who were the shoes for? In this whimsical world of Mr and Mrs Gadigun did the woodland creatures have tiny horses to ride around on?

When the time came to find a trade I decided to pluck up courage and enter the shop to ask Mr Gadigun for a job. I thought that an apprenticeship in taxidermy would allow me to continue my studies in biology and I could gain a thorough knowledge of anatomy.

With my field study books and box of mounted butterflies under my arm I one day went to Stonebridge and pushed open the door. I had prepared myself for an assault on the eyes as I expected to see all manner of grotesqueries: half-finished displays, dissected animals, &c. What I hadn't expected was an assault on the nose. With my first intake of breath I gagged and almost turned on my heel. The air was thick, as though I had taken a gulp of some foul liquid. The smell was not one thing in particular but a mixture of chemical, animal and sickly sweet.

The shop was dark and so crammed with objects that it took a while for my eyes to adjust.

I heard footsteps approaching from a back room and Mr Gadigun emerged through a door behind the counter. He was a small man with a perfectly round head upon which perched a light-coloured wig. His teeth protruded below his top lip and had large spaces between them, which meant that when he talked he whistled several different notes in harmony. He wore no jacket but a filthy leather apron over his smock and he peered at me over tiny spectacles clamped to the bridge of his nose.

'Aha!' he exclaimed. 'He's here!' I looked around to see if anyone else had followed me into the shop. Mr Gadigun leant back through the door and called, 'He's here, Frugal! The young gentleman has come!'

I was confused. 'Were you expecting me, sir?' I asked.

'Indeed, sir!' he whistled. 'We've been expecting you this last two years!' Again he

called into the back of the shop, 'Frugal! I told you he would come!'

Frugal, I came to realise, was Mr Gadigun's wife. (I later found out that she is one of five sisters who were each given the name of a desirable virtue. Honesty, Faith, Charity, Goodness and Frugality. I think Mrs Gadigun drew the short straw.)

'I don't understand, sir. How did you know I would come?'

'Because I see you every day! You never walk by my shop without looking in through the window. It stands to reason that you have been saving up your money in order to buy one of my displays. Don't tell me! Is it the weasel and viper? A fine piece though I say it myself, or maybe Mr Mole the blacksmith?'

'No, sir, though I am very taken with both of

those displays. No, sir, I have come to ask you for a job.'

Pansas Gadigun could not have looked more shocked had I announced that I was, in fact, King George III.

'A job?!'

'Yes, sir.'

'Here?!'

'Yes, sir.'

'Frugal! He's come for a job!' He turned back to me. 'Why then, boy, I am completely wrong! Instead of coming to give me money you are proposing to take money away from me!'

Though his manner was eccentric he was not unfriendly and I set about trying to convince him. I laid my book on the counter and flicked through some of my drawings and diagrams before opening up my box of butterflies.

'I feel I could be a considerable asset to your business, Mr Gadigun. I know a vast deal about the natural world and am keen to learn more. One day I wish to go to university and become a great scientist.'

Mr Gadigun carefully studied my drawings, the mounted butterflies and then my face. Suddenly he straightened up and said, 'Come!' and gestured for me to go around the counter, whereupon he led me into the back room of the shop. If anything the air was thicker and more pungent back here and it quickly became clear that this was where the work happened. There were three workbenches upon which sat three displays in various stages of completion: a stoat in a coat, a rook with a book, and a frog with a mandolin.

As I took in my surroundings Mr Gadigun

went to a cupboard and fetched out an object which he proudly set down on one of the surfaces. It appeared to be a circular polished wooden base such as many of his pieces were mounted upon, only this one was very small, about the size of a crown piece. He pointed to it.

'My most ambitious project to date!' he announced. He could see that I was confused and with a grin produced from behind his back a large magnifying glass, which he thrust towards me. 'Go on,' he urged, 'take a look!'

I took the glass and peered through. There, standing arm in arm upon the small wooden disc was a pair of fleas dressed in full wedding costume. Astounded, I looked up at the taxidermist.

'It is their wedding day!' he said with glee.

'Look again! Do you see Mr Flea's cane? And Mrs Flea's bouquet?'

It was extraordinary. Mr Flea was indeed leaning on a minute walking stick and his bride, dressed in silk and lace, carried a microscopic posy of flowers.

'Incredible!' I said. 'But how . . . ?'

'With these!' replied Mr Gadigun and held

out his hand to show me a set of miniature tools no bigger than sewing needles. 'I hold my breath as I work and, with much practice and great concentration, I am able to slow my heart rate. I can then time stitches and incisions between the beats of my heart which would otherwise jog me and make work impossible.'

It was a fantastic thing to behold and I told him so.

'Well, young Tooth, if you work hard at your studies and do as I instruct then you will one day produce such beautiful things.'

'You mean,' I said in incredulity, 'that I have the job?'

'Why yes!' he exclaimed with a B sharp. 'You shall be my apprentice! And I shall teach you all the secrets and tricks of the trade!'

And so I found myself apprentice to Mr

Pansas Gadigun the taxidermist and started my training the very next day.

Mother was predictably scathing about my choice of trade, saying that nobody ever became rich by stuffing dead animals. If anything this disapproval confirmed that I had made a good decision and spurred me on.

I threw myself into my apprenticeship and learnt quickly. Mr and Mrs Gadigun were kinder to me than anyone since Grandfather and oft-times I would sleep there under my workbench to save going home to that joyless house in Church Street.

When my mother died and I found myself homeless my employer happily welcomed me into his home and the workshop floor has been my bed ever since.

Friday 21st August 1772

I have been working in my spare time on a surprise for Mr and Mrs Gadigun for their wedding anniversary.

I wanted to make a stuffed griffin, a mythological creature from ancient Greece. A griffin had the body of a lion and the head and wings of an eagle.

I obviously can't get hold of a lion so I am making a baby griffin using a rabbit and a seagull. I have affixed cat's claws to the rabbit's feet and swapped its cottontail for that of a stoat (the closest match I could find in Mr Gadigun's box of tails).

I think they will be delighted.

Dined today of pigs' ankles and blancmange.

Tuesday 1st September 1772

Mr and Mrs Gadigun were less than delighted
with their stuffed baby griffin.

They gawped at it and Mrs Gadigun gasped. I sensed I had overstepped a line.

Mr Gadigun took me through to his workshop and explained, in a kindly manner, that there is an unwritten taxidermists' code which says that the natural world cannot be tampered with.

'There is such a rich variety of creatures out there in the world, Ben,' he explained, 'many of which have yet to even be discovered, that we have no need to try and improve upon or embellish nature.'

I told him that I understood, that I hadn't meant to offend, and the matter was over. Mr Gadigun went back to working on his water vole cricket match display.

Tuesday 29th September 1772

Today is my sixteenth birthday. Mr and Mrs
Gadigun made me a gift of a new set of scalpels,
an old volume entitled *How Humans Descended
from the Giraffe* and a magnificent display of a
stuffed fish at a weaving loom. A quick scan of
the book revealed it to be utter rubbish but it is
good to become familiar with these ridiculous
theories in order to then reject them.

Also today a most intriguing letter, addressed
to me, was delivered to the shop.

It is from a law firm in London and reads
thus:

D. C. Ounaloos & Cuck, Lawyers
10 Great Warner Street
Clerkenwell
London

Dear Mr Tooth,

May we congratulate you on the
occasion of your sixteenth birthday and
invite you to visit us, at your earliest
convenience, at our London offices
where we have some legal documents
that will be of interest to you.

Yours faithfully,

Mr Digby Charles Ounaloos &
Mr Archibald Cuck

What this means I have no clue and I will have to wait to find out. There is no question of me taking time off for a week or more as there are several urgent orders to finish.

The prospect of visiting the capital city is a daunting one. I have heard nothing but frightening reports of the place.

Today, as a birthday treat, Mrs Gadigun served cold eel pye with a baked pickle pork pudding.

Wednesday 7th October 1772

Today, amongst my various errands, I had to deliver a finished piece of work for Mr Gadigun. The piece, a beautifully stuffed spaniel puppy, had taken some weeks to complete and was to be taken by hand to a house in Stonebridge. It was only as I approached the house in Fishpool Lane that I thought to check the name of the customer. I was, at the same time, thrilled and horrified to see the name of my beloved Izzy Butterford upon the invoice. I had not seen her since I left Miss Ormeroid's dame school and though I love my job and my employers it is not the celebrated scientific world that I once boasted to Izzy I would belong to. I knocked at the door of a pretty cottage (exactly as I imagined it would be) and the maid showed me to a parlour room while she went to find the mistress of the house. As I waited I caught sight of myself in a looking glass. Journal, I looked dreadful. My hair was lank and greasy, my tatty clothes stained with all manner of grime. There was nothing I could do and no time to do it as the parlour door opened and in walked Izzy looking more beautiful and radiant than ever. She stopped in her tracks when she saw me and all but burst into tears. 'Benjamin? Is it you?' she said and I reluctantly owned that it was. 'But what has happened to you? Are you fallen on hard times? Have you come to ask for charity?'

I wished the ground could have opened up and swallowed me as I told her my circumstances and tried to persuade her that things weren't as bad as they appeared. I thought that she would be cheered that I had brought her puppy but this just made her sob at the memory of him. Things went from bad to worse as I tried to comfort her and she recoiled in horror with a 'Pooh! What on Earth is that revolting stench?!'

I have been living and working with Mr
Gadigun so long now that I have become
insensible of the smell but my clothes and
probably my very person are impregnated and
I take the essence of the shop around with me
wherever I go.

And so, having caused her horror, sorrow and
revulsion in quick succession, I decided to grant
relief and take my leave. I did not get to talk to
her as we used to talk. I did not find out what
she is now doing and it was with forlorn step
that I made my way back to the shop.

On the morrow I will ask Mr Gadigun for
an advance of my wages that I may buy a new
suit of clothes to wear when I travel to London.
I cannot present myself at a respectable city
lawyer's smelling like rancid ditchwater.

Thursday 8th October 1772

My guardian insisted that, rather than advance my wages, he would loan the money for a new outfit at no interest and to be paid back at my convenience. Mr Gadigun and his wife really are the sweetest (if not the sweetest-smelling) people I have ever met and I shall repay them a hundredfold when I am rich.

Mr Taylor the tailor measured me for new britches, vest and a coat of cobalt blue and also a shirt and stockings to be collected Wednesday next before I go to London. Then to Mr Lincolnsob the milliner for a fine tricorn hat. The hatter offered me a job but, apart from the fact that I am already happily employed, Mr Lincolnsob is as mad as a March hare and in all honesty, who wants to be a milliner? Last to

Mr Last the cobbler for shoes.

The problem will be where to store the new garments the night before and indeed where to change into them for as soon as they are brought into the shop they will assume the pungent air of that establishment.

The weather has been extremely warm all week for the time of year.

Dined tonight from the remains of last Sunday's fish pye.

Up all night with greatly disturbed stomach. Cannot think why.

Must be something to do with the full moon.

Wednesday 14th October 1772

Today I collected my new items from Misters Taylor and Last and secreted them in a hollow tree trunk by the millpond. I shall go there first thing in the morn to change before I catch the London coach.

Mrs Gadigun was upset not to see me in my new finery though I claimed modesty as the reason rather than the offensive smell of her good home.

Thursday 15th October 1772

I need not have worried about my smell. London is surely the most fetid place on Earth.

I rose before dawn and snuck quietly out of

the shop and to the place where I hid my new clothes. Once dressed I made my way out to the London road and waited for the morning coach.

There were two other gentlemen on the coach but not a word was spoken between us for the whole journey. As we approached our destination I called out to the driver to ask if I could sit up beside him and he agreed.

From the top of Highgate Hill I got my first view of London. Though the morning was fine and clear a sickly grey cloud hung over the city and flocks of screaming kites wheeled and swooped over a hundred church spires. As we got closer and the red-brick buildings loomed up, as the fields of Marylebone gave way to streets and houses, I found myself apprehensive. I had not considered the size of the place. I felt as though I were a mere flea on the back of a huge, stinking animal. Deeper into the streets we drove and deeper under the blanket of smoke. Traders were beginning to appear carrying baskets of wares and all shouting for custom with cries I could hardly understand. Small boys in filthy rags were running like ants between the legs of the traders, trying to steal a bun or a pye. Packs of mangy dogs were doing the same.

The streets were awash with slicks of oily mud in which floated putrid lumps of who-knows-what. The kites I had seen from the hill were all around, scavenging on offal and entrails thrown out of butchers' shops.

Some of the streets were very narrow but the coach driver plunged down them and left it to the pedestrians to dive out of his way. One street vendor was drenched head to foot with

greasy brown muck thrown up by our wheels and shouted such curses as would make a sailor blush. The coach driver found it hilarious.

We eventually reached Clerkenwell and I left the coach at Great Warner Street.

Immediately my new shoes were ruined as I stepped in something unspeakable.

With squelching stockings I made my way to the premises of D. C. Ounaloos and Cuck.

Upon entering the shop I found myself in a dark, gloomy hallway that served as a waiting room. A dozen or so chairs were placed around the perimeter and on one sat a tattered old gentleman without a hat who glanced up at me hopefully before returning to stare mournfully at his grimy hands.

I took this sorry heap of rags to be neither Ounaloos nor Cuck and so I sat and prepared to wait I knew not how long. The room was bare but for the chairs and a large clock in the corner that ticked and tocked monotonously and chimed the quarter hour. Throughout the morning I sat in that dingy room as the chairs gradually filled with a motley selection of Londoners. Each time the door opened we quickly raised our heads and then slowly lowered them again as another surly character shuffled in and took his or her place in line.

Eventually at almost one of the clock the street door opened and everyone bar myself leapt to their feet and spoke at once, accosting the stooped gentleman that entered in. Mr Quinaloos (for it was he) clutched a large bundle of ledgers and documents under one arm and held up the other for silence.

'Mr Thunder,' he said, pointing to a man

with a bloodied apron whom I assumed to be either a butcher or murderer, 'I have no news for you so you are wasting your time in coming here. Next Thursday, Mr Thunder, at the earliest.' Mr Thunder shuffled out muttering something under his breath. Mr Ounaloos then dealt with the others in similar fashion: 'Mrs Foothead, we are still looking, come back Tuesday week. Mr Singletary, until you can present to me some documentary proof I cannot help you with your claim to the throne of England,' and so on until the lawyer had dispatched all but the original ragged old man and me. He pointed first at me. 'You, sir!' said he. 'I don't know your face.'

'I am Benjamin Tooth,' said I.

'Tooth! At last! I thought you would never show! Come, my boy, we have to speak.'

He opened the inner door through to the back office and ushered me in, turning to the old gentleman as he did. 'You will have to wait, Mr Belch. I shouldn't be more than a few hours.' Mr Belch looked daggers at me as I went through and the door was closed behind me.

The office of D. C. Ounaloos and Cuck was a place that daylight never penetrated. The walls were clad ceiling to floor with shelves that groaned under the weight of countless books, papers and files. Placed in amongst these were unguarded candles that flickered and spat and threatened to set the whole place ablaze at any moment. Two large desks were set facing each other and behind one I was surprised to see a huge gentlemen fast asleep and snoring with his mouth open. Mr Cuck (for it was he) had apparently been there all morning whilst my new friends and I waited patiently on the other side of the door.

Mr Ounaloos rattled a poker in the fire grate by way of an alarm clock and yelled, 'Mr Cuck! We have a visitor!'

Mr Cuck hauled himself out of his slumber with much grunting and lip smacking, wiped the drool from his chin with the palm of his hand and blinked at me with a look of profound confusion. 'Mr Cuck, this is Master Tooth,' explained his colleague. 'Tooth, Cuck. Cuck, Tooth.'

'Tooth?' said Cuck.

'Tooth,' said Ounaloos.

'Oh *Tooth*!' said Cuck.

I proffered my hand and immediately regretted it as he grasped it in his, which was still glistening with dribble.

'A pleasure, a pleasure, my boy!' said he. 'We thought you'd never come!'

Mr Ounaloos in the meantime had been scouring a high shelf near the ceiling and, spotting the relevant file, now retrieved a folding stepladder from the corner of the room. Then, to my surprise, instead of climbing the ladder he held it above his head and knocked the ledger off the shelf, sending it clattering to the floor. He scooped up the scattered papers, dumped them on to his desk and settled himself in his chair. 'Please,' said he and gestured for me to sit.

'We have had,' began Ounaloos, 'in our possession this last ten years or more a letter from your father, Josiah Tooth, with strict instructions that you were to received it not a day before your sixteenth birthday.' With this he

placed on the desk in front of me a yellowing,
folded letter with a wax seal.

Mr Ounaloos leant over and, with his
fingertips, pushed the letter closer.

'Please,' he said, 'open it.'

I took up the letter, broke the seal and began
to read.

My dearest Benjamin,

It is with a heavy heart that I sit down to
write this letter, knowing that if you are
reading it then it means I did not return
from the Americas. I hope you will forgive
me for leaving you and know that my
only reason was to secure for my family a
comfortable future safe from the cold hand of
poverty. If you are reading this then I failed.

Perhaps I perished on the journey out,
perhaps I succumbed to disease or starvation
or to the elements. Whatever the reason, you
have lived for more than a decade without a
father and it is time to make some amends.

Before I left I placed in the trust of the

gentlemen lawyers, Mr D. C. Ounaloos & Cuck, a sum of money that, by the time you are of age, will have grown to a sizeable pension.

I have instructed the gentlemen that you are to receive from the age of sixteen the sum of two thousand pounds per annum until the pension is gone. You are to use this as you see fit and with no restrictions only that I pray you will use it wisely.

Also, on the occasion of the death of your dear mother, the house at Church Street will become yours.

Your loving father,
Josiah Tooth
Wednesday 10th June 1761

I stared at the page and read it slowly through once more until a loud snore brought me back to the room where Mr Cuck had fallen once again into a deep slumber. Mr Ounaloos, his chin resting on his fingertips, was observing me closely.

'Well, Master Tooth,' said he, 'may I congratulate you on your new-found wealth and present you with this,' he handed over an envelope, 'the first instalment.'

In the envelope was a crisp bank bond made out to the value of £2,000. I was all but speechless and only managed a stuttering 'Thank you' before making my way out of the office with instructions to return in twelve months, past the hapless Mr Belch, and finding myself back on the bustling streets of London, richer than I could have imagined.

My reverie did not last for long. I walked into Ray Street and as I passed by Pickled Egg Walk I suddenly felt someone seize me from behind. A hand clamped itself over my mouth and dragged me back into the alley. Though I could not see my assailant's face, from the smoothness of the skin and the waft of stale bergamot I knew this was somebody I had encountered before. I was pushed into a doorway and spun around to face a grimacing Farley Cupstart who held me fast, at arm's length, by the throat.

'Well?' he hissed. 'Where is it?'

'Where is what?' I choked.

'You know what!' His pale eyes were manic. 'My property! That is what!'

'I don't know what you mean!' I protested but once again he tore my satchel from my shoulder and spilt the contents on to the filthy cobbles.

He then roughly checked my coat pockets before sinking to the ground with a mournful wail and holding his face in his hands.

'Time is running out,' he whimpered. 'I must have it before it is too late!'

'If you could tell me what it is you are looking for then I might be able to help you,' I offered, and he looked up with desperate eyes.

'What I showed you!' he moaned. 'What I drew for you those weeks ago on Windvale Moor!'

'But you've never told me what that drawing *meant*, what it's meant to *be*, and it wasn't weeks ago, it was *years*!'

'Years?'

'Yes!' I cried in frustration. 'Four or five years ago.'

'It can't be,' he murmured. 'Years? Time goes so fast. All is lost, all is lost.'

'And you destroyed my house!' I could feel the anger bubbling up inside me as the pathetic figure sobbed into his hands. 'And you destroyed my family! So tell me what I am supposed to be looking for! Tell me what is this thing that is so important to you!' Now I grabbed him by the throat and he looked up terrified at me.

'I am weak!' he gasped. 'You'll kill me!'

'Tell me!' I was now seething with rage.

'It is gone!' His voice was now no more than a whisper and all strength seemed to have drained from him. 'It is lost. Gone. All hope is gone.'

I left Cupstart whimpering in Pickled Egg Walk and turned north, wishing to escape the mayhem of the city. Before long I found myself surrounded by fields and pastures. Presently I came to Bagnigge Wells where many well-dressed people were gathered in beautifully manicured gardens along the banks of the Fleet River. I paid my shilling and entered. I wandered for an hour or more through the borders and walks, past fishponds with stunning

125

orange fish and genteel musicians who played sweetly in the autumn sunshine. The contrast of the tranquil gardens to the cacophonous pandemonium of the city was a breath of fresh air (although the Fleet River has its own unique fragrance) and there I found some peace and quiet to contemplate my new fortune and what it meant for my future.

I decided that the first thing I must do is to pay back Mr Gadigun and buy myself out of my apprenticeship. I have learnt much from him but know that, now my situation has been improved, I do not want to follow him into the taxidermy trade.

When the time approached to meet the coach back home I decided to walk further north and intercept it on the road rather than return to the city at dusk. This I did and arrived back in

Stonebridge a little past nine of the clock.

And so I find myself at my workbench above
the piece of floor that has been my bed for
the last four years. I will work out my month's
notice with Mr Gadigun and then start on
renovating the old house in Church Street that
has fallen into dereliction since Mother died
and it has been empty. Mrs Gadigun wept
bitterly when I told them I was leaving and
made me promise to visit often, saying that I
was the son she never had.

My head is bursting with possibilities but
there are two things I know I must achieve
before anything else. Firstly to secure a place
of study at university.

Secondly to ask for the hand in marriage of
Miss Izzy Butterford.

Sunday 1st November 1772

I have been reading a lot about the ancient art of alchemy. Alchemists of the past have been able to turn common substances into precious metals. But they told no one of their methods and the secret has been discovered and lost several times.

I think I know how to do it.

I have to deduce the individual ingredients and the quantity of each needed to make gold. To work out the exact combination will require a dedication.

After many hours of careful thought I have discovered that gold consists of five different elements: blood, fire, water, honey and a sense of foreboding. I have made several attempts, the only product of which was a foul-smelling grease, which I have yet to find a use for.

The sense of foreboding is hard to muster when I am so excited by my work.

Dined tonight of the scrag end of a neck of mutton with potatoes boiled and a cucumber.

Monday 23rd November 1772

I have been back in my old home in Mereton for a week. The years of my absence have not been kind to the old place. The death-watch beetles have eaten all the chairs and the smell of damp is all-pervading.

I tracked down Eleanor, our old maid, and asked if she would consider resuming her post as housekeeper.

After a week of work we have rendered the house habitable once more and some new items of furniture arrived yesterday.

The plaster and paint on the front of the house is crumbling and peeling but I shall wait until the spring to start work refurbishing the exterior.

Wednesday 24th March 1773

Two things happened today of great and puzzling significance.

I awoke to read the following piece in *The Gazetteer and New Daily Advertiser*:

Mysterious Death in Westminster

Yesterday was found in Dean's Yard, Westminster, the body of one Farley Cupstart, a gentleman of no fixed abode and belonging to no parish.

Mr Cupstart was found standing bolt upright with a smile upon his face but stone cold and rigid, as though he had been quite dead for a number of hours. There were no marks upon his body and no clue as to cause of death. The deceased had the appearance of a young man though papers found about his person revealed him to be three and ninety years of age. Many are claiming witchcraft and sorcery as the cause of his death but officially it has been recorded as 'old age'.

So that disturbing and sinister personage has gone from my life and I feel a weight has been lifted from my shoulders. Though he has left many questions unanswered, it certainly fits that he was older than he seemed to be. He frequently referred to a time when he knew my great grandfather 'many years ago', which he could not have done if he had been the age he appeared.

As if that piece of news were not enough for one day, the townsmen who are stripping and refurbishing the outside of the house have uncovered plasterwork above the door of a design that set my blood racing. It was mid-morning when I went out to inspect their work and just in time as they were about to pull down a circular plaque about a yard in diameter.

At first, though I recognised it, I could not recall where I had seen it before. But then with a rush of wonder I realised it was the same image that that scoundrel Farley Cupstart had sketched on a piece of paper on Windvale Moor all those years ago. The same image that had set in motion a chain of events leading me, for better or worse, to where I am now. I remembered sketching the image in my journal. I ran inside to find it.

There is no doubt in my mind that the two images represent the same thing.

So is the plaque what Cupstart was looking for? I assume not, as he could not have thought I had a large plaster relief hidden about my person or in my satchel. So this must be just another representation of whatever he was so desperate to get his hands on.

I am almost certain that Grandfather must have made the plasterwork and put it there many years ago before I was born but I am still no nearer understanding what it means. Nor do I know the next step to unravelling the mystery. Cupstart is dead and Grandfather, I must assume, is the same.

Thursday 25th March 1773

I awoke early and, with the news of Farley
Cupstart's demise still fresh in my mind,
decided today was the day to start my life in a
new and positive direction. I felt that destiny
was smiling upon me and resolved to take
advantage of that good fortune and ask Izzy
Butterford to marry me.

I dressed in my London clothes and set
out to Stonebridge, stopping along the way to
gather an armful of Izzy's favourite hedgerow
flowers. The sky was such a shade of blue and
the spring breeze so warming on my skin that I
felt the world was on my side and there was no
way she would refuse me.

Oh, Journal, how wrong I was.

As I crossed the green towards Fishpool Lane

who should I spy sitting under an old walnut tree but Izzy? And who should I spy sitting next to her and holding her hand? Well, Journal, it wasn't me. I felt as though an arrow had pierced my heart as I saw Izzy smiling happily up into the face of some village idiot who presumed to take my love from me. I was so struck with grief that I just stood and stared until the intruder noticed and whispered to Izzy, whereupon she looked up and came skipping across the green.

'Benjamin!' she cried gleefully and threw her arms about my neck. 'How wonderful! I have been thinking about you this past two days!'

I opened my mouth to speak but no sound came out.

'Benjamin, you'll never guess!' (I already had.) 'I'm to be married!' My world came crashing down around my ears.

'Come and meet him, Ben, do!' and I found myself being dragged by the hand to the fateful tree to meet my enemy. 'And you'll never guess!' Izzy continued as she dragged, though I was in no mood for guessing games. 'His name is also Benjamin! Isn't that too funny?!' I admitted that it was about the funniest thing I had ever heard and found myself standing before him. He remained sitting on the bench and looked me up and down with an air of amusement.

'And who might this be?' he asked and it was all I could do to prevent myself socking him in the eye.

'Benjamin my love,' said Izzy (to him), 'this is also Benjamin, my dearest friend in the world!!' Again he looked me up and down.

'Shake hands, *Benjamins*!' said Izzy, enjoying the extraordinary coincidence. 'I just know you are going to be the closest of friends!' Knowing the opposite and struggling against every instinct in me, I pushed my hand towards him. He looked at it and then reluctantly offered his own. It was like grasping a dead fish and I suppressed a shudder, struggling not to then wipe my hand on my britches.

'Benjamin is to be a doctor,' she said, referring to the chinless booby, 'and we are to live in London while he studies.' If my heart could have broken any more it would have done at that moment.

'Nice flowers,' said the young man, pointing at the bouquet at my side. 'Who are they for?'

'For you,' said I.

'For me?' said he.

'No, I mean for Izzy,' and I handed over the flowers. 'Congratulations to you both.'

'Then you knew!' she cried and again threw her arms around me, much to the obvious annoyance of her beau. 'You are such a complete darling! You must come to the wedding!'

I muttered something about 'wouldn't miss it for the world', offered my congratulations once more and turned to face a miserable walk back home.

On the way back I tried to kick a chicken but missed and fell hard on my rump. It feels bruised but I can't see and I'm certainly not asking Eleanor to look.

All is not lost. I can still win back my Izzy.

I have discovered that her wedding is to be delayed until her betrothed has qualified as a doctor. All I have to do is qualify before him

and make my name as an eminent scientist.
I shall start in earnest on the morrow.

Wednesday 26th May 1773

I have come to the conclusion that I was born
in the wrong age. My intellect is too advanced
to be appreciated in this time and will only be
seen for what it was in future centuries when
humanity catches up with me.

Not long after my last diary entry I started
in earnest writing letters to the heads of all the
major colleges in the land, telling them of my
brilliance and my wealth and even including
examples of some of my private studies. From
the majority came no reply whatsoever, not even
an acknowledgement of receipt. Those that did

respond sent short and humiliating rejections.

No matter. I need not the help or guidance of those imbeciles and will continue my work unaided and unfettered by their narrow minds. I will take my findings direct to the people. I will publish independently and sell wisdom door to door.

An Experiment: I have heard it said that if one stops washing one's feet, after several weeks they start to clean themselves. Apparently the natural oils in the skin begin to cleanse the feet and they eventually become sweet-smelling and silky smooth.

I shall experiment by bathing one of my feet as normal and leaving the other unwashed.

Thursday 3rd June 1773

I am still haunted by the mystery of Farley
Cupstart and my grandfather and have exhausted
all avenues of investigation. I am convinced that
I will find the answers on Windvale Moor and
spend all of my spare time in that lonely place
searching for a sign. However, it takes the best
part of a morning to travel to the moor and I
have decided that I need a more permanent base
there from which to conduct my search. There
is a ruined farmhouse on the moor just north
of a narrow, clear-running brook. It has, by its
appearance, stood empty for many a year and so
I have made an application to buy the ruin and
the acre of land on which it stands.

Abed early with Earwax.

Monday 14th June 1773

A bothersome ghost is frightening the maid.
The spectre of John Brickett (who was master
cook to King Henry VIII) is oft to be seen
sitting in the chair at the foot of the stairs. Or,
rather, his wig and occasionally his clothes
appear in the old oak chair that once belonged
to that gentleman.

(Mr Brickett was burnt at the stake for burning the King's steak and it seems I purchased his ghost along with his chair.)

Apparitions bother me no more than mice, they are merely a nuisance, but Eleanor is terrified of the thing and refuses to sweep the stairs or hallway.

My ginger cat keeps the mice at bay but seems greatly fond of Mr Brickett, oft-times curling up in his spectral lap.

I shall turn my thoughts to a ghost trap.

Dined today of a giblet, boiled with raisin and currant suet pudding and turnips.

Friday 18th June 1773

After some experimentation I constructed the below in order to capture Mr Brickett's ghost:

The trap uses a large sponge squeezed into a tight ball with leather straps. When the trap is sprung the straps are released allowing the sponge to expand to its full size at a gradual and controlled rate. This slowly draws the apparition into the porous structure and holds it therein.

I positioned myself in the hall with a twine

in my hand and after a wait of perhaps an hour and thirty minutes I witnessed the spectre descending the staircase and making himself comfortable in his chair. Thereupon I pulled my twine and watched as his ghostly garments were sucked into the sponge. A job well done.

Dined of a sheep's head, cold with greens.

Saturday 19th June 1773

After last even's successful experiment, and in my haste to get to bed, I left Mr Brickett in his spongy prison next to the kitchen basin and forgot about him.

In the morning Eleanor took my sponge to clean her own house and, in wringing it out, inadvertently released Mr Brickett's none-too-happy ghost.

I can't say I'm too upset. Serves her right for nicking my sponge.

Wednesday 7th July 1773

Today I heard that my offer on the old farmhouse on Windvale Moor has been accepted. I shall start work immediately on its restoration.

Tuesday 20th July 1773

Results of Self-cleaning Feet Experiment:
I found that the foot I stopped washing on

26th May got progressively dirtier and more smelly until the cheesy odour started attracting flies and mice.

I therefore conclude that feet do not clean themselves.

I shall publish my findings in a pamphlet.

Wednesday 20th October 1773

Work has almost finished on the house that I have bought on the moor.

I have decided to carry out an extensive survey of the flora and fauna of the moor and I will be able to move my books and equipment in in the coming days.

I have named the house 'Tooth Acre'.

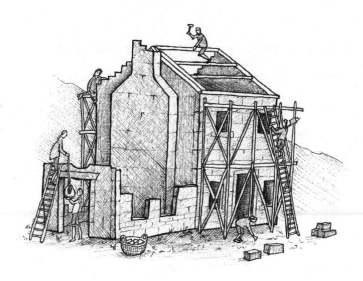

Saturday 23rd October 1773

Exciting reports this morn that a large ape has
been washed up on the beach at Inglesea. I will
travel there presently and see if I can procure
~~the beast. The opportunity to study such an~~
animal would be incredibly interesting and I
understand that they can, with patience, be
tamed and become good companions.

Later

My efforts to acquire the shipwrecked ape
were sadly unsuccessful. Arriving at Inglesea
it was not difficult to find the whereabouts of
the creature and I was directed to a local tavern
where it was being held in a narrow back room.
A small window in the door offered views into
the room and people were paying a shilling to
peer in. The beast was, as I suspected, a young
chimpanzee. I enquired as to who had brought
it in and was introduced to two nasty-looking
characters at a table who were greedily counting
their takings. On my asking if I might purchase
the chimp of them they became quite aggressive
and told me of their plans to tour the animal
from town to town and make their fortune.

I decided on a new approach, and when the

local sheriff arrived I casually suggested that the ape could be a French spy sent to gather military information. I told him that I would be happy to take the animal with me and extract information from it. This suggestion did not have the desired effect and instead the rumour started to circulate that this was not a chimpanzee at all but a hairy Frenchman and that more were on their way. The sheriff clapped the poor creature in irons and carted it off to jail.

So I have returned empty-handed. The people of Inglesea really are quite the most foolish people in the land.

Saturday 30th October 1773

An irritating piece in *The Gazetteer and New*

Daily Advertiser this morn:

Idiot Yokels Imprison Monkey

Wednesday last, at Inglesea, a large monkey was found washed up on a beach. The beast was captured and soon a sizeable crowd had gathered to gawp and jeer.

A local Inglesea man, one Benjamin Teeth, claimed the creature was an invading Frenchman and, on his insistence, it was locked in jail and tried as a spy.

Mr Teeth is due to collect his prize for the Stupidest Man in England from the King Tuesday next.

The following 'humorous' illustration accompanied the text:

The Nincompoop of Inglefea
(The man, not the monkey)

the confuſed monkey for a Frenchman.

Never have I been so enraged. For a start
a chimpanzee is not a monkey but an ape.
Secondly my name is *Tooth* not *Teeth* and
thirdly I am not and have never been from
Inglesea.

Monday 1st November 1773

This even an angry mob of twenty hammered
on my door brandishing a copy of the *Gazetteer*
and demanded to know what I meant by
making a laughing stock of the town. I pointed
out the mistakes in the text but this didn't seem
to wash with them and they were at the point of
barging their way into the house when Justice
Wooten arrived and they began to disperse.
They made it quite clear, though, that I am

no longer welcome in Mereton and so I shall move permanently to the moor. Not because they have driven me out but because I no longer want to be associated with nor live in a town of such dunderheads.

Part the Third

Sunday 17th May 1778

My name is Benjamin Tooth. This is my journal.

It has been near five years since last I wrote.

But I have not been idle. On the contrary, I have built up a vast body of work.

My isolated existence on Windvale Moor suits me to a T and I will oft go days or a week without encountering another living soul. The lack of such distractions has allowed me to concentrate on inventing numerous herbal remedies, machines and contraptions. I have mapped the moor beneath my feet and the heavens above me.

Shortly after I moved in I converted the large downstairs room into a laboratory and it is there that all my fieldwork is collated and written up.

I am quite certain that never has a more complete and exhaustive study been made of any other habitat on Earth as I have made of this landscape. To the untrained eye the moor would appear a desolate and sparsely inhabited wilderness but nothing could be further from the truth. The wealth and diversity of both plant and animal species is astonishing. Indeed, on certain summer days the air is so thick with life, a living soup, that one feels like wearing a face mask for fear of inhaling a lungful of invertebrates.

A great deal of my daily intake of food (though I don't need much) comes from my foraging trips on the moor and surrounding countryside. I have learnt which plants are edible through a system of trial and error. My errors early on caused many an uncomfortable

night of stomach cramps and one particularly
distressing occasion led to me cutting all fungi
from my diet.

These days I live off a rich and varied menu
including many edible leaves, roots, seeds
and berries, honey from my hives, hazel and
beech nuts, birds' eggs, snails and sloes. My
trusty blunderbuss will bag me a hare or rabbit,
partridge or grouse and the stream offers up
eels, crayfish and sweet brown trout. Other fish
to be found in the brook include gudgeon and
miller's thumb but these are small and bony and
taste of mud.

Occasionally I will make a trip to the
coast and spend the day collecting shellfish,
crabs and shrimps, various types of seaweed
and armfuls of bitter sea kale. I think I have
never been in such good health and the clean
bracing air and lack of butter and coffee in my
diet have given me an energy and zest for life
that I never experienced whilst living in that
ungrateful town.

The only times now that I need visit
Mereton are when I require supplies that
cannot be gathered from nature: scientific
instruments, paper and writing materials,
&c. On the rare days that I do visit town I
take with me medicinal potions and printed
pamphlets of my scientific findings, which
I sell from door to door. The people of that
town though are a superstitious bunch and

view me as some wandering mountebank or witch doctor rather than the learned scholar that I so clearly am. I have a few regulars, however, who are always interested in my findings: Mad John Long the wheelwright, Crazy Terry the miller's boy and Mr Lincolnsob the hatter are among my most loyal customers. (John Long is a keen amateur vintner and usually pays me with a bottle of his latest wine. You would be surprised (and taken aback) at the things Mad John can make wine from.)

I do have two occasional visitors out here on the moor. The baker's boy from the nearby village delivers essential supplies once a week: bread, milk and cheese, and if he has cause to travel to Mereton he will pick up my post and deliveries.

I have never asked his name but he is quite the most dim-witted Jack Pudding I have ever met. His hair is dense, matted and black and grows so far down his forehead that it looks like a strange hat. He has one thick eyebrow from under which tiny eyes glare accusingly. He has the overall appearance of a miniature, prehistoric cave dweller.

Once, as he was putting my supplies in the larder, I told him that there was a sheep on the roof. He dropped everything and ran outside to see, then returned a few minutes later with a glum expression and told me that it was no longer there and must have flown off.

Hatty Pepper is a travelling tinker woman who criss-crosses the country selling her wares and who passes this way every three months or so. She is small and weatherbeaten, of gypsy origin I think, with large rings in her ears and on her fingers, and a great mess of hair piled up on her head like a chicken's nest. Hetty sells all manner of interesting tat and it is always a cheery day when I hear her cart clanking and jangling down the track towards Tooth Acre. Last time she came I purchased of her three bear traps, an old cavalry sword and a bishop's mitre. She always turns down the offer to stay overnight in the house and instead sleeps under her wagon in the garden, but not before we have sat up and she has regaled me with tales of her travels and the divers people she has encountered. She is most stimulating company.

Monday 13th July 1778

Today as I was paddling in the brook and looking under rocks for crayfish I found something that set my mind a-thinking. Clinging to the leaf of a bulrush was the empty shell of a dragonfly nymph. Nothing unusual in this as I have oft seen them before and, indeed, last summer spent an enjoyable afternoon watching a beautiful hawker hatch from its larval clothes and dry in the sun before taking flight across the moor. The specimen I found today, though, was much larger, perhaps twice the size of any I have seen before.

This discovery has awakened in me a memory. Many years ago, when I came to the moor to look for the warbler that I raised and released, and again on the sad day that I

found my grandfather's clothes abandoned,
I remember sighting at a distance two huge
dragonflies, quite the largest I had ever seen.
Could this be the nymph of that elusive species?
I am convinced of it and, if I am right, it is
surely a species that has never before been
described.

Monday 20th July 1778

Dreamt last night that I was eating a tough-skinned baked potato.

This morning I can't find one of my shoes.

Friday 31st July 1778

Today as I was bathing in the brook I spotted on the bank what I first thought to be a giant snake. At over two yards in length and of a dark brown, almost black coloration, I knew it was not one of my friends the adder or the grass snake and feared it to be some venomous cobra or the like. I climbed out of the water and edged cautiously closer only to discover that it was a fat female eel slithering like a serpent across the grass. There have been no great storms of late, the river has not burst its banks, so I can only conclude that the fish left the water by choice. I followed it for some distance before I suddenly remembered that I was stark naked and though it would have been easy to catch (I had nothing planned for dinner) I decided to let it go, so intent was it on getting wherever it was going. It seemed to be heading towards the sea. An enigmatic creature, the eel. I have never witnessed them spawning and wonder whether this gravid hen fish was off to a secret breeding ground.

Curiously, when I returned to my clothes where I had left them by the brook, all of the buttons and buckles were missing. Had somebody been spying on me and played a joke? Was it a thieving jackdaw? It is a mystery.

Sunday 2nd August 1778

A revelation!

For the past fortnight I have been thinking constantly of those huge dragonflies and the nymph case I found at the brook. Something has been niggling at my brain like a *déjà vu* or a half-remembered dream.

Today it struck me.

There is a striking similarity between the nymph and that strange design that I saw first in

Farley Cupstart's drawing and then again in the plaster relief above the door at Church Street.

After all these years I feel as if I've stumbled upon the beginnings of an answer to that infernal mystery, though I am still a long way from solving it.

Did Grandfather discover this creature first? He was certainly a keen explorer and interested in many things. He was a knowledgeable man and had learnt a great deal about natural history. So how was Cupstart involved? He, I am sure, was not an accomplished naturalist. Did he mean to gain from Grandfather's discovery? Had they ever really been friends? Somehow I doubt it.

Next step? To find this giant dragonfly.

Dined today of hot oyster porridge.

Thursday 13th August 1778

Today when the baker's boy arrived with my
supplies I decided to try to inspire him with my
work. As I explained my drawings and described
the complex environment of the moor he fell
quiet and I thought that I had fanned the spark
of his imagination. But when I turned to look
I found him studiously picking his nose with
great focus and concentration.

I fear he will never be my student and protégé.

No matter. His skills at delivering bread are
beyond compare.

Dined of a bowl of ox-tripes and hogg's
pudding.

Abed early with the Belching Sickness.

Christmas Day 1778

I have seen one! At long last I have seen one
of the great dragonflies I have been searching
for. However 'dragonfly' seems hardly an
appropriate nomenclature any more, for what
I saw is something quite different. As in my
previous sightings, years ago, I only spotted this
specimen from a distance and would possibly
have not given it a second glance but for the
time of year.

It is midwinter and Windvale Moor is carpeted with snow to a depth of several feet. The brook is frozen over, the trees are bare and the black gorse, itself blanketed in ice, is the only visible vegetation. What on Earth is a dragonfly or any other insect doing flying at this time of year? No, this was not an insect, this was no cold-blooded creature. This is something entirely different, entirely new.

I am close, I can feel it. Close to making the discovery of a lifetime.

New Year's Day 1779

Another sighting. Again infuriatingly distant but unmistakable. This one was skimming across the south face of the downs, occasionally dipping

to touch the snow in a movement similar to
that of a damselfly laying its eggs in a pond. But
though it moves in a similar way to an insect
its movements are too deliberate, too thought-
out, as if searching for something, not randomly
darting and zigzagging like a dragonfly.

It was not two hundred yards from the spot
where I saw the other a few weeks back and not
far from the brook where I found the nymph
shell last summer.

I shall set up some sort of hide close to this position and keep watch.

Friday 15th January 1779

The best sighting yet! And so astounding as to be almost unbelievable. This time there were two of them and closer than before. What I saw I almost hesitate to write down as it would seem utter madness to anyone reading it. Journal, these were not insects, they were, my hand is shaking, they were tiny *people* with wings! There, I am finally going mad. My isolation on the moor has turned my brain to lime jelly. And yet I am positive that is what I saw. Tiny people, no more than six inches tall, with dragonfly wings, looking for all the world

like . . . no, I can't bring myself to write it.
I must go and lie down.

Later

As I lay on my bed trying to clear my brain and
think straight about the day's events I heard my
grandfather's voice in my head. It was a memory
from my childhood and a time when he would
tell me stories to send me to sleep. He told tales
of a race of miniature people with wings who
lived peacefully in a far-off place. I always took
these tales to be inventions of Grandfather's
imagination but the more I think of it now the
more I am convinced that he knew of these
creatures on the moor.

Saturday 16th January 1779

I shall not use the F-word in this journal
or in my field report book. It is vulgar and
unscientific. Suffice it to say that these creatures
resemble a popular mythical creature that oft
features in children's stories. I shall think of a
different word to describe them.

Sunday 17th January 1779

The two creatures that I saw were frolicking
and playing, chasing one another, and looked
to be positively enjoying themselves. I may be
mistaken but through my telescope it appeared
they were throwing snowballs at each other.
At one point, though, they stopped their

gambolling and seemed to become aware that
I was watching. After looking in my direction
for a few seconds they took fright and in a flash
they were gone.

This again is not the behaviour of an insect.
The hawkers and darters that hunt on the
moor during the summer months seem all but
oblivious to my presence when on the wing.
True, when they are at rest on a bulrush it is

difficult to get close but when they are flying they will head straight towards me and only change direction at the last instant. The timid nature of the playful two is more akin to a mammal or bird.

In the past, when observing other wild animals I have found patience to be the best virtue. Sitting still and in the open, the subjects eventually become accustomed to one's presence and if they feel no threat they will become steadily more courageous, making observation easier. Therefore I have decided to abandon my hide and from now on brave the elements so they become used to me and know that I mean them no harm.

Wednesday 3rd February 1779

'Sprite' is the word I have decided upon to describe this new creature. It still invokes regrettable images of the mythical or supernatural but for now, until something better occurs to me, they shall be known as sprites.

Sunday 7th February 1779

I now think that both Grandfather and Farley Cupstart knew of the sprites.

Grandfather's interest, I'm sure, was scientific but Cupstart would only have been concerned with personal monetary gain. Maybe he discovered Grandfather's secret. Perhaps he blackmailed him.

Another thing that I cannot ignore is that both men lived to an unnaturally old age. I feel sure this is a factor somehow in the mystery.

A light snack before bed of lardy cake with egg and butter gravy and pig-syrup suet dumplings with cream.

Friday 19th March 1779

At last today I felt the first welcome breath of spring in the air. These past two months of staking out the moor in the bitter cold and driving rain have taken their toll on my health and I have the weatherbeaten appearance of an old saddle. With not a single sighting since the two I spotted in mid-January I at times have come to think they were a figment of my imagination. But I will keep faith for if what I saw was as astounding as I believe then I may be close to an Earth-shattering discovery.

If nothing else I have been able to observe the changing of the season in such detail that I sometimes feel I am part of the fabric of the moor itself and have an affinity with the grass, the furze, the rocks and the hills. I may even pen a poem.

Monday 22nd March 1779

A visit from my travelling friend Hetty Pepper. It is always good to see Hetty's cheerful face and today was no different. She climbed down from her cart vigorously scratching in her tangled hair and laughingly told me that she was 'crawlin' with vermins such as is driving me to distraction'.

I, of course, was delighted as this gave me an opportunity firstly to try out my new Eel-cheese Embrocation for the Expeditious Expunction of Cranial Parasites and, secondly, to collect some specimens for my collection.

Living within the jungle of Hetty's hair I found no fewer than six different species:

> Common Lice
> Head Worms
> Noggin Ticks
> Bonce Flukes
> Scalp Limpets
> and, most surprisingly of all:
> Mistletoe

As I explored the uncharted territories of Hetty's head I questioned her on the subject of 'little people' and whether she thought there were any such things. It did not surprise me that she had a lot to say on the topic and though she had not seen any herself she told me tales of people she had met that strongly believed in their existence.

'I once sold a kettle in Kilkenny to a man with a beard of bees,' she began, 'who, before bed each noyt, would throw his shoes across the room. Every mornin' when he awoke the shoes had been polished to a glorious sheen by the pixies who lived in the well.' She continued with extraordinary stories of elves, goblins, trolls and of the Hidden Folk of the Icy North that live in rocks. All of these though are magical, mystical beings that, whether or not they really exist,

seem far removed from my moorland sprites.
The sprites are not mystical or supernatural,
they are wild animals striving, like every other,
to survive.

Hetty made me a present of a stargazy pye that
we ate with a dish of radishes.

It was a fine and handsome pye with seven
different types of fish baked within. Their heads
poked through the crust, gazing heavenward,
which made the pye not only flavoursome but
amusing.

Tuesday 30th March 1779

My patience has paid off! Today at last I have
sighted two sprites, possibly the same two as I
spotted previously. But this time I felt sure they
were aware of my presence and though they
did not get close they certainly did not flee as
before.

Wednesday 31st March 1779

Two sightings in as many days! An individual
this time. Again it looked briefly in my direction
but then carried on skimming the grass and
seemed not worried by me. It headed off over
a ridge to the south as the others before have
done. I think perhaps that this is where their

nest (colony? hive?) may be found but I must resist the urge to move my position until they are completely comfortable with my being a feature of the landscape.

Tuesday 20th April 1779

For the past two weeks I have sighted sprites almost every day and have started to move my position forward, by no more than a yard, each morning. In this way I am slowly edging towards the spot where the creatures usually first appear and then eventually return.

Using my telescope I have been able to observe them for a few moments at a time and will now offer my first tentative description.

I described them early on as looking like 'tiny

people with wings'. Though this reads as rather crass it is, incredibly, still accurate.

I think I have observed at least five different individuals.

They have four limbs, two arms and two legs, though the legs are greatly elongated and seem to act as a tail for balance and changing course when in flight. I have only ever seen them on the wing and wonder whether they are even *able* to walk or stand. The legs certainly appear too long and fragile to support even their slight weight.

They have darkish, olive-coloured skin, two large eyes and, as far as I can make out, four slender wings. At least two of the individuals I have seen appear to have some coloration at the wing tips, perhaps an 'eye' as on a peacock feather.

Thursday 3rd June 1779

As the days go by and the sprites become more accustomed to me I have become bolder in moving my position forward. I am now camped on the crest of a hill and can see where the colony appears to be based. It is a large, shallow hump of ground with several, perhaps ten, entrance burrows that looks as though it may have once been a rabbit warren.

My appearance at the top of the hill obviously caused some concern as I subsequently went five days without a single sighting. They have now started to appear again but are wary and tend to fly off in the opposite direction from me. Through careful observation I think I have identified the location of a possible second colony half a mile to the north-east. I shall investigate this further before taking any steps closer and risking them becoming suspicious.

Saturday 19th June 1779

I have taken to wearing a pair of antlers when watching the sprites on the moor and further, I have started to pull up and munch on handfuls of grass. Though this behaviour may sound odd it is designed to put them further at their ease. Horned beasts, though they may look fierce, are generally herbivores and so pose no threat to other living things. If the sprites believe I am some sort of strange, bipedal grazing animal they will soon learn to ignore me.

I have even perfected a repertoire of snorts and grunts, which I emit at intervals.

Wednesday 30th June 1779

Either I am losing my reason or there is a thief
on the moor. Due to my early starts I will often
have a short sleep in a sheltered spot. On three
or four occasions I have woken to find some
small item missing, my watch chain (but not my
watch), for example, and the amber hatpin that
I use to winkle snails from their shells.

My suspicions immediately settle on the
baker's boy. There is something about him
I don't trust. I think it's his hairline. Or his
unbroken eyebrow. Anyone with a forehead that
narrow must be up to no good.

I must leave myself a reminder to beat the
boy next time he comes.

Friday 9th July 1779

My ungulate disguise has been working well
and I have managed to approach much nearer
the warren because of it. That was until Tuesday
last when the sprites suddenly fled inexplicably.
I continued to snort and chew mouthfuls of
grass for a while until I heard the sound of
jeering and laughter. A group of furze gatherers
had assembled on a nearby hill and were
watching me with great amusement. I wanted
to shout abuse at them but, afraid of blowing
my cover, I just shuffled off towards home,
occasionally braying like a donkey to the delight
of my spectators and howls of mirthful laughter.

As if this was not irritation enough, more
people came the next day to see the spectacle
and the day after that even more still. On the

fourth day the word had spread and quite a crowd had gathered, many with picnics, to see the 'madman of the moor'. I tried to ignore them but eventually they started throwing stones. No doubt some of them had travelled from Mereton to ridicule me.

Their opinions do not matter in the least, I care not what any of those maggots think of me, but my research has had to stop until they get bored and go away. I just hope it does not take too long before I can regain the trust of the sprites. I fear the progress I have made may have been damaged and I have taken a few steps backwards. Dash those imbeciles.

I am so irritated I fear I may be coming down with the Green Sickness.

Thursday 22nd July 1779

Today, trusting that my audience had forgotten
about me and moved on, I ventured back on
to the moor to resume my watch. My fears
about the sprites' trust in me turned out to
be completely unfounded. Indeed, the whole
affair seems to have had the opposite effect.
No sooner was I back in my place and grazing
on the vegetation as before than a group of
eight or more sprites came out as if to welcome

me back. They came much closer than they have in the past and if I'm not much mistaken they seemed to show sympathy. It was as if they had witnessed my being driven from the downs, had seen the rocks being hurled at me, and decided that I was a harmless animal being persecuted.

So I have the last laugh. Those stupid townspeople have helped me on my path to fame and fortune.

Monday 2nd August 1779

It is time for my research to enter its next phase. I have shown great restraint and self-control in the past months, resisting the urge to attempt to catch a specimen and concentrating instead on gleaning all the information I can about their behaviour from afar.

I have identified five different sprite colonies, or tribes, on Windvale Moor and mapped their locations.

I call them:

Brook Tribe: This is the original colony I became aware of down by the stream.

Crag Tribe: These occupy a large warren under a rocky outcrop about a mile north of the brook.

Gorse Ring Tribe: This colony lives in a network of burrows completely enclosed by a dense circle of gorse bushes. So uniform is the barrier that I suspect the vegetation was cultivated especially for the purpose of defence. The gorse is very old and gnarled, suggesting it was planted many generations ago. I consider this tribe to be the oldest and largest of the five.

Plains Tribe: These sprites, though certainly a colony, seem to occupy scattered, temporary rabbit holes and are of a more nomadic nature. They did not appear on the moor until the warmer months, suggesting that they have travelled from their wintering grounds.

Northern Tribe: These live on the most northerly reaches of Windvale Moor. A little further north and the landscape becomes farmland.

Each colony contains, by my estimation, between thirty and fifty individuals. They are social animals forming close relationships, 'friendships' almost, with fellow members of their colony.

I have sensed little rivalry between the tribes. Parties of three or more individuals will oft visit a neighbouring warren, where they are greeted by a welcoming party and invited in.

I have noticed slight differences in appearance between the populations. The sprites in the Northern Tribe, for example, have darker hair on their heads, while those in the Plains Tribe tend to have colourful wings. This could be evidence of subspecies or perhaps individual tribe identity. Perhaps they colour their wings using dyes or paints.

The sprites' diet remains a mystery to me. At a guess I would say they are generally omnivorous, eating a variety of seeds, berries and insects. They are constantly foraging in the gorse and grass and down by the brook but I cannot get a clear enough view to see what they have been gathering. When they do find something they will fly straight back to the nest, which suggests that they share their food with the rest of the colony.

I have now gathered as much information as I think I can without capturing a specimen and conducting a closer examination.

The baker's boy came today but I completely forgot to beat him. Next time.

Wednesday 18th August 1779

On Experiments in Trapping Techniques

My first forays into capturing a sprite have been unsuccessful. I have tried a variety of methods: spring traps of the type used for catching thrushes, wire snares, even glue traps where I have smeared sticky resin on likely perches.

All have proved useless in the catching of sprites, the trouble being that I do not yet know what the beasts feed on. Those spring traps I baited with honey remained set, those I laced with flying ants catch'd meadow pipits. No matter, I shall dine on pipit pudding and ponder the problem further.

Wednesday 22nd September 1779

I have abandoned my disguise of late and, as
such, spy the sprites less frequently.

   I know where they live, though, and so
long as I am careful not to get too close I am
confident they will not abandon their colonies.

Tuesday 16th November 1779

For the first time since leaving the house in
Church Street and moving out here to the moor
I have started to feel pangs of loneliness. It is,
I am in no doubt, because of the importance
of my discovery, the excitement of each new
development and the lack of anyone to share
it with.

I have written to Izzy Butterford in London. That sweet, if misguided, girl is the only person in the world that I would willingly share this information with and I know she would be as thrilled as I at the chance to study an entirely new species. I remember how, as children, we sketched and painted flowers and butterflies. I remember how they seemed to trust her and would linger in her presence. Izzy would be my ideal companion in work and life and she could help me with my work if she were with me now. In the letter I did not disclose exactly what I have found, lest it should fall into enemy hands, but hinted at the immensity of the discovery. Izzy is a ~~country girl. She does not belong in London, she~~ belongs here with me on the moor. If she has not been corrupted by that city I know she will come and join me. I anxiously await her reply.

Tuesday 29th February 1780

I have been successful in trapping almost every
creature present on the moor except those
infernal sprites. Weasels and stoats, mice and
voles, birds, insects, everything but a sprite.
I think they must be highly intelligent and
suspicious of any contraption that looks out of
the ordinary. But they must have a weakness,
and I will find it. I need to capture a specimen
and I care not any more whether it is living
or dead.

Wednesday 12th April 1780

I awoke this morning incensed with anger
and frustration at my inability to capture one

of those blasted sprites. Before I could think sensibly about what I was doing I took up my blunderbuss, loaded it with buckshot and stormed out on to the moor.

I had not gone more than a few paces out of the garden when I stopped: should I go back and put on my antlers? I would not stand a hope of getting near enough to one of the creatures without wearing them. As I turned to head back a small bird flew past me and alighted on an elder tree close by. The bird, to my astonishment, looked to be the very same species of warbler that Izzy and I had once raised and released on the moor. Without a moment's hesitation I swung the gun to my shoulder and 'BLAM!' I pulled the trigger. A puff of feathers and the bird dropped to the ground. I ran over and there it was, without

doubt identical to the bird from all those years ago. I had all but forgotten about it.

The bird was damaged from the shot but not out of all recognition so I gathered, as best I could, the loose feathers from the grass and took it inside. The rest of the day was spent happily preparing the skin of the tiny bird to be stuffed the way Mr Gadigun taught me as a youth.

And so in leaving the house determined to capture one creature new to science I succeeded in bagging another equally unknown, though perhaps not quite so sensational.

I'm sure Izzy and I gave the fledgling a name but for the life of me I cannot remember what it was.

Friday 21st April 1780

This even as I was heading back across the downs towards home I heard the familiar jangling music that heralds the arrival of my old friend Hetty Pepper and her cart of treasures.

I soon spotted her coming over the hill and we walked back to the house together. I had not had a chance to hide away my work and so hurriedly gathered my papers and stuffed them into a drawer as she settled herself by the fireplace and stirred up the embers.

'And what might this be, Professor Tooth?' (She calls me 'Professor'. I have no formal qualifications but it would seem churlish to correct her.) She was holding a piece of paper that I had overlooked in my haste to clear up. It was a drawing I had made a year or more ago, comparing the strange nymph that I found at the brook to the design on the plaster relief at Church Street.

'Oh, that's nothing,' said I, 'just a study of a dragonfly larva.'

'Well 'tis handsome strange, Professor,'

continued the tinker, 'as I've seen a likeness of this a month ago, made in silver, not far from Steerborough on the coast.'

My ears pricked up though I tried not to appear too interested.

'Oh yes?' said I.

'Most certainly, Professor, I'd swear to it, but what I saw was not a scribblin' like what you've made here but a hornament.'

'A "hornament"?'

'That's royt, a hornament, a little statue about yey high,' she held her hands to show me something about six inches tall, 'and 'twas made in silver.'

I could hardly contain my excitement.

'Where did you see this?' I asked. 'Where was this statue?'

'Why, Professor, I bought it in a box of old

bric-a-brac, bits and pieces, none of it any value except for that one piece.'

'And where is it now?'

'Ah, Professor, I sold it on, couldn't even tell you who bought it. I was selling my wares at a fair by the new windmill on the marshes, not far from where I picked it up. No doubt somebody took a shine to it, pretty as it was.'

'What else,' I asked, 'was in this box?'

'Well now, let me think.' Hetty sat back and rubbed her forehead. 'There was papers, you know? Old papers with writin' on which I used to light me fire (being as I can't read), some old-fashioned clothes what I tore up for rags, and, let me think . . . Ah! I remember! There was something else which I saved, thinking as it may be of use to you!'

With that she jumped up and went outside

to her cart where I followed her. After much scrabbling about and poking in her many boxes and baskets of junk she pulled out an old brass telescope.

'There!' she said triumphantly. ''Tis one of them hinstruments what makes the small things bigger, you know? Brings the faraway things closer.'

How Hetty Pepper came to buy the effects of Farley Cupstart I shall probably never know, as she could not recall where she had picked them up, but I had no doubt that I was now holding that gentleman's battered telescope, for engraved upon the side were the initials *F.C.*.

I offered her half a crown for the glass but she refused, saying that I could have it by way of rent for letting her stay the night.

So. A silver statuette. Is that what this is

all about? But if this ornament was already in Cupstart's possession, what was he looking for?

Perhaps he believed my grandfather owned a second one.

After much mulling over of the evidence I have come to the following conclusions:

1. There were two statues.
2. Farley Cupstart was in possession of one of them, which was made of silver.
3. Cupstart believed that Grandfather had the other.
4. Cupstart believed that the two together held great value or power.

Wednesday 10th May 1780

At last! I have captured a live specimen! The people of Mereton will rue the day they ever hounded me from their stinking town. I shall be rich!

First things first: to give the beast a name. Pending a thorough internal examination I have provisionally classified it as a new species of the *Homo* genus displaying characteristics of the *Odonata* order of insects. Therefore it shall be called *Homo insecta Dentii* (the latter for myself) but it shall be known as the Windvale Sprite.

The trapping method that eluded me for so long was, as is often the case, so simple as to be laughable. I soon found from my observations that there are two things the creatures cannot resist:

1: Any crack or crevice, ditch or dyke they can't help but explore. (They live, from all I can gather, in old warrens that the rabbits have either abandoned or been chased from, as I was from Mereton.) 2: (And this is the thunderbolt!) Shiny things! Be it a new penny or a shard of broken glass, if it reflects the sun they want it and will go to any lengths to get it. My discovery was made thus:

Two days ago, whilst keeping my heathside watch I happened to drift off to sleep in the afternoon sun. I was presently awoken by a buzzing sound and on stirring surprised two of the creatures who made off with great haste across the moor. I looked down to discover three of my silver coat buttons gone, the thread bitten through. Stolen! It was only then that I thought back and remembered other items mysteriously vanished: a shoe buckle, a watch chain and my amber hatpin. All no doubt pilfered by those winged rapscallions.

But they are sly! Or clever, for when the traps were obvious they stayed away, sensing danger, and anything mechanical or sprung they would steer clear of.

And the solution was a bucket. A mere bucket from my yard, baited with a silver sixpence, sunk into the ground with a heavy lid propped up on a stick that I pulled away on a twine.

The first two attempts brought them close but they sensed or smelled me and fled. Working on the theory that they have an extraordinary sense of smell, on the third attempt I endeavoured not to touch any of the components of the trap with my hands and wrapped my feet in wads of grass lest my footprints should carry my scent.

And that was the key! I waited 'til it was inside and tweaked the twine from my position downwind. The lid came down and the prize was mine.

Once back in my lab I transferred the specimen into a glass-fronted box and took some sketches and observations. I have concluded that the creature is a male of the species. He has light, silvery hair on his head and extending, like a lion's mane, down to the shoulder blades, from which sprout four large wings. From high on the forehead, right on the hairline, extend a pair of long, club-shaped antennae similar to those of a butterfly. Its eyes are large and compound, dark blue in colour. The skin is tough and leathery, reminding me of the exoskeleton of a crustacean. It will be interesting to dissect it and see whether it also has an endoskeleton.

On each hand are four fingers and an opposable thumb. They do not have fingernails but instead are tipped with a wispy thread. Each foot is divided into two large toes.

On the side of the arms, from wrist to shoulder, and up the back of each leg, from above the ankle to the top of the thigh, runs a line of short spines.

Wednesday 17th May 1780

Two more specimens captured ruby.

One of them looks very young, perhaps only recently hatched from its nymph.

The other is considerably older with large

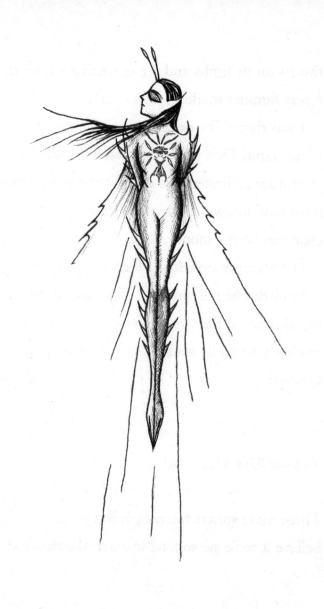

thorns on its limbs and, I can hardly believe it, a very familiar marking on its chest.

I was right! The design above the door, the silver statue, Farley Cupstart's sketch and the sprites are all linked. What is more, Grandfather must have known about the existence of the creatures on the moor.

His bedtime stories were true.

Why did he tell only me? Why did he not reveal them to the world? Why did he live modestly when he could have been rich and famous?

Tuesday 23rd May 1780

Three more sprites trapped. I find it hard to believe it took me so long to catch the first and now they fall for my traps three at a time!

These three are my first from the elusive Plains Tribe.

Absent from the moor during the winter months, the Plains Tribe are harder to trap as they tend to move about and never settle in one place for long. All three have coloration on the wings and have adorned themselves with pieces of jewellery fashioned from seeds, feathers and tiny bones (possibly from a shrew).

All are equipped with a vicious sting, as I have experienced many times to the detriment of my poor nerves. A barbed thorn at the base of the ankle administers the venom, which is painful but lasts no longer than a bee sting. The animal can twist its body wildly though, and sting even when you think you have a good grip on it. These days I wear leather falconry gauntlets whenever I handle them.

The sprites are infuriatingly nervous and skittish. I have to remain very still when sketching as any sudden movement will send them into a violent frenzy, dashing themselves against the bars of the cage and tearing their wings in the process.

Tuesday 30th May 1780

A Note on Housing and Feeding

The creatures are best housed in small birdcages of the type used for finches. No cover need be provided as this encourages them to hide and makes observation impossible. They prefer to cling to a vertical branch rather than a horizontal perch but their wings are best displayed when the cage is left bare and they must cling to the bars.

A water bowl may be provided but one need not offer food, as the creatures will not feed in captivity.

Pondering how best to profit from my discovery I have come up with an idea. Thinking of the time in Inglesea and how those two rogues profited from a shipwrecked chimpanzee, I remembered just how willingly the poor townsfolk gave their shilling just to get a look at the beast. Imagine how easily they could be parted from their money to see a sprite! I could charge a guinea and people would be queuing down the street.

I started thinking of a tour around the country, setting up in town halls or at fairs. To make it more of a spectacle I thought of teaching the sprites to perform or to wear tiny clothes. However, this would be impossible at present. They are so timid and terrified when I am around that I doubt whether they can be tamed.

The memory of dear Mr Quilgud's stuffed animal displays has inspired me to think up ways that I can put the sprites in human situations for the amusement of an audience.

A Note on Pickling and Preserving

Though I continue to try to keep one of the creatures alive for a period they rarely last three or four days before their refusal to eat and their self-harming tendency makes them useless for experimentation. Therefore it makes sense to kill the specimens as shortly after capture as possible so as to preserve them in a prime physical state.

They can be dried and pinned out as one would a large insect. I have achieved this a number of times but the body shrivels somewhat and loses shape as it dehydrates. Also the skin darkens in colour.

Salting does not work as the exoskeleton is

impervious to salts and the insides continue to decompose.

Pickling is the best of a bad selection until I find some better method. A solution of formaldehyde, water and methanol in a half-gallon jar will keep a specimen indefinitely but all colours fade to a uniform yellow-grey within a matter of weeks.

Saturday 1st July 1780

The puzzling question of Grandfather's and Cupstart's great ages and how this relates to the sprites has been occupying my thoughts. The symbol tattooed on their skin is without doubt the key.

Those that bear the markings appear to be

older than those without and several seem to be of a very great age indeed. I have counted the growth ridges on the exoskeleton of a particular individual and calculated it to be at least one hundred and fifty years old.

I will concentrate my efforts on the Brook Tribe that inhabits the old warren by the stream. All of the marked specimens I have collected came from the vicinity of this nest so I conclude that the answer to the mystery will be found there.

Monday 3rd July 1780

I have started digging on the south-facing bank. It is hard work and I could use some help but I'll be damned if I shall share this discovery with even the lowliest labourer.

Tuesday 4th July 1780

I have been stung by the spiteful little beasts
one too many times, and have lost all sympathy
for and patience with them. Tomorrow I will
go to town and purchase some ferrets with
which to drive them from their burrows. Then
I can continue to excavate without risk of being
constantly stung.

Wednesday 5th July 1780

The ferret plan worked as well as I could have
wished. After securing nets across every hole I
could locate I sent down the two animals who
were eager and hungry. Almost immediately
the sprites started to flee and were trapped:

I netted a dozen good specimens of varying ages. Unfortunately I seem to have missed a hole on the northern side of the warren and soon witnessed a mass exodus of perhaps a hundred individuals who flew in a swarm away across the moor to the north-west. A breakaway group must have doubled back, however, and I was stung severely several times on the buttocks as I tried to coax the ferrets back out.

Once they were gone I lost no time and began to dig.

The entrance tunnels are extraordinarily deep and only after two hours' solid work did I come across a first 'room'. A small dugout containing nothing but a pile of acorn cups. A stockroom perhaps? There are no oaks on the moor so they must have been gathered from far afield, perhaps used for bowls or drinking vessels. I progressed another couple of feet downwards before the tunnel started to level out to horizontal. It began to get dark and though I was tempted to return to the house and get candles to work through the night, the wind was starting to pick up and the clouds threatened rain. Before I left I barricaded the hole securely with stones and rubble to prevent the creatures returning to their home and stealing any of their possessions back.

A further three or four feet along the passageway I fancy it starts to open up into a much bigger chamber. I shall return at daybreak

Thursday 6th July 1780

I have found it! The object that the creatures
hold in such high esteem and which I am
certain has some kind of mystic power of eternal
youth. It is mine!

I'll be brief as I have many dissections to
perform on the captured specimens and they are
dropping like flies.

When I returned to the warren at first light
there was indeed some evidence that a group of
them had been back to salvage their treasures
but the rubble barricades were too much for
them. They had started to dig new tunnels
down but they had been abandoned, probably
as they saw me arriving.

It didn't take long to reach the room I
mentioned yesterday, some sort of dining

hall with earthen tables and benches in rows.
Other rooms and antechambers lead off this
hall, dormitories perhaps, but nothing of great
interest was found here.

It was then I realised that the fresh tunnels
that had appeared overnight were on the other
side of the mound. Whatever they were so
desperate to retrieve was obviously on that side.
I started to dig in the direction of these new
holes. After an hour's hard graft the ground
suddenly caved in and revealed a large chamber
filled with objects, the collected treasures of
generations of sprites. They were the shiny
trinkets that I have come to know the beasts
cannot resist. Lots of junk and scrap metal,
spoons, nails, stained glass, and my stolen
coat buttons and hatpin, all polished to a high
sheen. But amongst the rubbish are many

valuable items, numerous coins, some of them gold, dating back to Roman times, small pieces of jewellery and gems. I shall spend many enjoyable evenings sifting though my hoard, grading and valuing the treasure.

The floor of this grand 'hall' (though it is, in actual fact, no bigger than the size of my pantry) had semicircular earthen ridges radiating out from a central point, presumably seating, and at the centre was the object of my search. A figure, a totem fashioned not of silver but in wood, perhaps rose or holly, barely eight inches tall and exactly as represented in the tattoos the creatures bear which have intrigued me so greatly. It is a beautiful piece of work with carving so intricate it can only have been rendered by tiny hands but, more than that, as soon as I grasped it and tore it from its base I felt an invigorating wave of health and vitality pass through me. The aches and cramps of the previous day's exertion evaporated and I felt as strong as an ox.

This wild place, this unforgiving Windvale Moor that I have come to love, has finally rewarded me.

A possible plan is to grind the statue to a fine powder and use it in potions that will guarantee long life and health. This I will sell at great profit, not to ordinary people but to Kings and Queens, only the very rich, and then so shall I be. It cannot fail.

There is a tap at the window. Is it Hetty Pepper? I did not hear her wagon . . .

It seems as though I have been tricked. Having locked the statue in my safe box I went outside to investigate a tap-tapping at the window. Finding nobody there I made a circuit of the house to check for intruders. Again finding nothing, I came back inside and bolted the door. Only then did I notice the specimen cage had been broken open and all twelve sprites awaiting dissection were gone. Sprung from jail! Perhaps I have underestimated these creatures. If they can plan and execute an escape from prison they must be more intelligent than I thought! Fascinating!

No matter, for I have as many preserved sprites as I need to present to the Royal Society and know of four more colonies should I need live specimens.

There is the tapping again! They shall not fool me a second time! Where is my gun?!

Friday 7th July 1780

I am barricaded in the basement of my house,
writing by candlelight, swollen and sore from
stings too numerous to count. They attacked
me! The ungrateful swine attacked me in my
own home!

On hearing a second tap at the windowpane
I leapt up, loaded my shotgun and went to
the door to listen. Hearing no movement, I
opened the door a crack and they were upon
me! Twenty or more of the things flew in my
face and batted around my ears. I stumbled
back, wheeled about and discharged the
blunderbuss into the room. I didn't hit a single
sprite but instead shattered the front window
whereupon dozens came swarming through
the broken pane and dozens more down

the chimney. I was surrounded by an angry, buzzing cyclone of sprites and felt the intense burning as they stung me on the ears, neck and hands. I turned the gun around and, using the stock like a cricket bat, I flailed about the room hitting out blindly, though the flying demons were too nimble and dodged each swipe with ease.

Suddenly I noticed that while the swarm attacked, another group had seized the statuette from my desk and were struggling to lift it up to the window. With a primal war cry I lunged towards them, hurled myself across the desk and grabbed hold of my prize. They could burn the house down for all I cared at that moment but they would not take the statue from me. Once I had hold of it they backed off (perhaps afraid that I would damage it), and taking up my cavalry sword I battled my way out of the room and down into the cellar where I secured the door and all possible routes in.

For a while I could hear them buzzing outside the door and frenetic movement in the house above but after half an hour it subsided and all was silent. I sat awake all night but must have drifted off to sleep around sunrise. I know not how long I slept for I haven't a watch or clock down here but the fear that they are up there lying in ambush has kept me prisoner in the basement the whole day. About an hour ago I heard a knock at the front door. I imagine this was probably the baker's boy bringing my order from town. I am hungry and thirsty and will have to venture out. I will be cautious.

All is lost! Sprites! Sprites! Sprites!

I have been beaten and I have no fight left in me to retaliate.

On leaving the cellar, statue in one hand and sword in the other, I ventured carefully up the steps, fully expecting a winged attack to come at me around every corner and from every shadow. The house was quiet save for the wind whistling through the broken window in the laboratory. At first it all looked as I had left it last night in the heat of battle but as I began to right the furniture and gather the scattered papers I noticed things missing. The sprites had been busy. Every specimen I had collected had been taken. Those I had dried had been prised from their mountings, cases opened, pickling jars smashed and the preserved specimens gone. Not a single one remains.

Furthermore, the locked box that contained all the treasure collected from the Brook Tribe warren had been broken open and the contents taken. The only physical evidence of their existence was the wooden statue that I held in my hand.

Outside the front door on the step was the basket of bread and supplies left by the baker's boy and atop it a letter the sight of which grieved me still further. It was the letter I had written to Izzy, returned unopened. On the back was a note explaining that Mrs Viggers (née Butterford) and her husband Dr Benjamin Viggers had left England and emigrated to the newly United States of America. Their exact whereabouts were unknown and so my letter had been sent back, with compliments, to Church Street.

I threw the letter on the fire and as I watched it burn I heard a voice. It said my name clear and gently: 'Benjamin Tooth'. The voice did not come from a direction but was all around me and within me, ringing like the chime of a bell. I turned slowly and there, hanging in the air in the middle of the room, was a single sprite. But this was no ordinary sprite (if such a thing is possible) and its like I had never seen before. It was large, perhaps half as big again as any I had witnessed, and instead of legs its lower body tapered to a beautiful swallowtail with vivid eye-markings at the tips. Its wings and the thorns on its arms were elongated into fine filaments which rippled in the air as though underwater. On its chest was the familiar tattoo.

It reached out its arms towards the statue in

my hand and again I heard the strange crystal voice: 'This belongs to us'.

I felt a knot of anger and injustice rising inside me. 'No!' I shouted. 'I found it, it's mine! It is all I have left!'

The voice came again, calm and clear. 'It does not belong to you.'

'It does!' I screamed. 'It does belong to me and you will never take it back!' and I darted to the table where I had left the sword and swung it towards the sprite. Despite its many tendrils and tails it was as nimble a sprite as any I have seen and easily dodged my blade, moving up to the ceiling and out of reach.

'Never!' I cried, incandescent with fury against the sprites, against the people of Mereton and Inglesea, against the universities that spurned me, and against Izzy Butterford.

'You will never have it back, I will burn it before I give it back to you!' and I moved towards the fire. It hesitated as if weighing up whether I was serious and then, in a move almost too fast to see, it was gone through the broken windowpane. I went over to my desk and sat down heavily, thoroughly exhausted.

I sat a long time. I poured myself a glass of Mad John Long's bacon and elderberry wine (but only took one sip for it tasted foul, like damp gloves and sealing wax) and thought about what was to be done.

Here is what I have concluded:

The light is gone from me and my anger is evaporated.

That the Grand Sprite spoke to me, not in audible words but by using some mysterious energy, means there is more to them than even I had imagined.

I have discovered, in these strange and beautiful creatures, a jewel of the natural world. The only way to keep that jewel safe is to keep it a secret. The more that know of their existence, the more likely the sprites will suffer the fate of the dodo a hundred years ago.

I will leave the Windvale Sprites in peace. I have been cruel and they deserve no more persecution from me.

But I cannot return the statue. I must keep it and use its powers to bring some good to the world. It grants long or even eternal life, I am certain of this, but what other powers of healing might it hold? Just to be in its presence might cure disease.

For too long I have been chasing the wrong

thing. Fame and adoration is not the answer, but to further mankind's understanding of this fragile orb that we have been granted lease upon.

So where do I go? I am not welcome on Windvale Moor or in Mereton.

I will follow Izzy to America. There I will reinvent myself and, with the aid of the statue, make my fortune and found *my own* university. The New World is mine oyster and I have all the time on Earth.

I will make a completely new start, take nothing with me. I have packed all of my collected works into my trunk and have left a note for Hetty Pepper to have it transported to Mereton and left to the people of that town. Once I have done writing this entry I will put the journal with the rest and hide the key within the body of the stuffed warbler (which I will also donate to the town) for whosoever is clever or stupid enough to find it.

But now I am tired. I cannot risk the sprites taking back the statue so I will sleep in my chair in the basement. Only a short nap. There is much to do.

This was the last entry in Benjamin Tooth's journal.

The silver statuette belonging to or stolen by Farley Cupstart has never been found. Some say it never existed, others that it was melted down not long after it was bought from Hetty Pepper. A few say it is hidden somewhere in the English countryside and that the clues to its whereabouts are to be found within the pages of The Lost Journals of Benjamin Tooth.

Read on for an exclusive first chapter of
The Windvale Sprites

Shortlisted for the
Waterstones Children's Book Prize 2011

1

The Storm

When Asa Brown thought back to the actual
night of the storm he found he couldn't really
remember it very well. He'd had a busy day
previously and had fallen into bed exhausted.
There he slept fitfully through noisy dreams
of howling beasts and old steam trains until,
eventually, he was woken by the sharp rap
of a stick hitting his window. He vaguely
remembered peering through the curtains but
not being able to see anything clearly. It was so
dark, unusually dark, there were no streetlights,

no cars on the road and the rain was coming straight at the windowpane. He lay back down and listened, for a while, to the tempest.

The raging wind was playing the houses and trees like the instruments of an orchestra, producing extraordinary noises. It whined and whistled, changed direction and dropped an octave, turned to the window and rattled the glass. Then it dropped silent for a second and crept back across the road to start again. Each time the wind slammed into the  house it seemed to get louder until it reached a crescendo, when a terrifying bass note would kick in and make the house vibrate to its very foundations. Beneath this noise, Asa could make out the smashtinkle of greenhouse glass and toppling terracotta pots, with fence panels and gates banging out an idiotic rhythm.

Strange though it might sound, these noises eventually lulled him back into a deep sleep. The house was old and prone to making unearthly noises, which he was used to and the drone of the wind was not unlike being on a train. So he went back to dreaming of locomotives thundering through tunnels and slept that way until morning.

The next morning was calm by comparison. The hurricane was now a mere gale and was carrying out its final checks, seeing that everything was dislodged that could be dislodged, uprooted or simply repositioned.

Many power lines across the area had been blown down and so, as there was no electricity, school was closed. Asa lost no time in exploring the damage outside.

There was a large pampas grass deposited in the middle of the lawn like a giant, stranded jellyfish. It had probably been blown there from Mr and Mrs Singer's front garden at number 72. A television aerial was trying unsuccessfully to get a signal at the top of the Hawthorn.

Then he saw it. Floating amongst the duckweed at the edge of the fishpond was a small figure. Asa assumed that it was a toy that had been blown from somewhere else, why wouldn't he? But as his fingers closed around it he jumped back in horror for what he touched was not plastic or wood. It was skin.

He sat down with a bump on the wet grass with his back to the fishpond and tried to calm down. His heart was pounding and he felt shaky. Thank goodness there was nobody around to see him, he thought, he must have looked pretty silly. Slowly he turned back to the pond and looked over the tall iris leaves.

There it was, floating face up just a few feet away.

It had big eyes. Huge black eyes that were all pupil. It was skinny like a stick with extraordinarily long legs that were bent back unnaturally. Its slender arms ended in delicate hands and fingers that tapered to fine points.

It was hard to tell exactly how tall it was but it couldn't have been more than six inches long.

Asa crawled closer.

The creature had olive-brown skin with a seam of sharp-looking thorns running up the outside of each limb. It had dark wispy hair on its head from which sprouted two long antennae and pointed ears.

As Asa looked more closely he could see that the surface of its eyes were made up of countless facets that glittered in the light. The tiny face had a sharp chin and framed a small nose and an even smaller mouth. On the creature's chest was tattooed a design like a Celtic knot and its skin was covered in bruises and scrapes.

With heart thumping, Asa dipped his fingers into the water and underneath the creature. It was all he could do to stop freaking out as he lifted it out of the pond and deposited it on the bank, quick as he could.

It flopped on to its front on the grass and Asa saw, with amazement, that sprouting from its shoulder blades were four, slender, transparent wings. An intricate network of veins divided each like a stained-glass window.

That is when the thought struck him. *I've found a fairy.* Just like that with no exclamation mark.

It's dead, but I am almost certain that I have found a real-life dead fairy. It suddenly all made sense. This is what 'fairies' are. Not wand-waving Tinkerbells but sinewy insect-men: wild creatures that must be very secretive and hardly ever spotted. This one must have been blown in the hurricane from the remote place where he lived and ended up in my fishpond.